She found herself staring at his mouth again, fascinated.

Cam must have noticed the direction of Maddie's gaze, because he said, "Did I leave any evidence?"

Maddie didn't know what possessed her, but she raised her hand, resting the palm lightly against his cheek, and with the pad of her thumb pretended to brush away nonexistent crumbs. He leaned forward slightly and so did she, bringing their faces into surprisingly close proximity. Neither she nor Cam moved. Her hand still rested on his cheek, and his eyes were clouded with some indecipherable emotion. They seemed frozen in time, the only two people on the planet, until he finally closed the gap and gently settled his mouth over hers.

Maddie had been kissed before. But this was like being struck by lightning—quite simply, nothing else compared. He tasted like dill...and heaven.

Dear Reader,

Summer's finally here! Whether you'll be lounging poolside, at the beach, or simply in your home this season, we have great reads packed with everything you enjoy from Silhouette Romance—tenderness, emotion, fun and, of course, heart-pounding romance—plus some very special surprises.

First, don't miss the exciting conclusion to the thrilling ROYALLY WED: THE MISSING HEIR miniseries with Cathie Linz's *A Prince at Last!* Then be swept off your feet—just like the heroine herself!—in Hayley Gardner's *Kidnapping His Bride*.

Romance favorite Raye Morgan is back with *A Little Moonlighting*, about a tycoon set way off track by his beguiling associate who wants a family to call her own. And in Debrah Morris's *That Maddening Man*, can a traffic-stopping smile convince a career woman—and single mom—to slow down…?

Then laugh, cry and fall in love all over again with two incredibly tender love stories. Vivienne Wallington's *Kindergarten Cupids* is a very different, highly emotional story about scandal, survival and second chances. Then dive right into Jackie Braun's *True Love, Inc.*, about a professional matchmaker who's challenged to find her very sexy, very cynical client his perfect woman. Can she convince him that she already has?

Here's to a wonderful, relaxing summer filled with happiness and romance. See you next month with more fun-in-the-sun selections.

Happy reading!

Mary-Theresa Hussey

Mary-Theresa Hussey
Senior Editor

Please address questions and book requests to:
Silhouette Reader Service
U.S.: 3010 Walden Ave., P.O. Box 1325, Buffalo, NY 14269
Canadian: P.O. Box 609, Fort Erie, Ont. L2A 5X3

True Love, Inc.

JACKIE BRAUN

SILHOUETTE *Romance*®

Published by Silhouette Books

America's Publisher of Contemporary Romance

For my true love, Mark.
Here's to happily ever after…

SILHOUETTE BOOKS

ISBN 0-373-19599-0

TRUE LOVE, INC.

Copyright © 2002 by Jackie Braun Fridline

All rights reserved. Except for use in any review, the reproduction or utilization of this work in whole or in part in any form by any electronic, mechanical or other means, now known or hereafter invented, including xerography, photocopying and recording, or in any information storage or retrieval system, is forbidden without the written permission of the editorial office, Silhouette Books, 300 East 42nd Street, New York, NY 10017 U.S.A.

All characters in this book have no existence outside the imagination of the author and have no relation whatsoever to anyone bearing the same name or names. They are not even distantly inspired by any individual known or unknown to the author, and all incidents are pure invention.

This edition published by arrangement with Harlequin Books S.A.

® and TM are trademarks of Harlequin Books S.A., used under license. Trademarks indicated with ® are registered in the United States Patent and Trademark Office, the Canadian Trade Marks Office and in other countries.

Visit Silhouette at www.eHarlequin.com

Printed in U.S.A.

Books by Jackie Braun

Silhouette Romance

One Fiancée To Go, Please #1479
True Love, Inc. #1599

JACKIE BRAUN

began making up stories almost as soon as she learned how to write them down. She never wavered from her goal of becoming a professional writer, but a steady diet of macaroni and cheese during college convinced her of the need for a reliable income. She earned her bachelor's degree in journalism from Central Michigan University in 1987 and continues to work as an editorial writer for a daily newspaper. Fiction remains her first love. She lives with her husband and son in Michigan.

CONFIDENTIAL

TRUE LOVE, INC.
Madison Daniels, President

Client Information—CONFIDENTIAL

Name: Cameron Foley *(Goes by Cam)*

Sex: Male *(Very, very male)*

Age: 36

Height & Weight: Six feet tall, 180 pounds *(Judging from the fit of his clothes, probably all muscle)*

Physical Description: Athletic build, light brown hair, brown eyes *(Cocky grin reminds me of Dennis Quaid)*

Marital Status: Widowed, three years ago *(Lonely? He says no, but I think he is)*

Children: Caroline, age six *(Absolutely adorable! He seems to be a devoted father)*

Occupation: Cherry farmer. Owns Foley Cherry Farm.

Health: Excellent *(Very physically fit)*, nonsmoker *(Thank goodness)*, social drinker *(Likes French wine!)*

Dating Preferences: Looking for a woman who is in her early 20s, tall, voluptuous, with blond hair and great legs. No divorcées. *(In other words, look for a woman who is my complete opposite because that's exactly who Cam Foley wants...or is it?)*

Chapter One

Cameron Foley was mad—no, more than mad, furious. And he allowed his temper full rein as he shoved open the double plate-glass doors that were etched with two large, overlapping hearts. A young woman, probably a college student, sat at the receptionist's desk just inside True Love, Incorporated's lobby, cracking her gum, head bobbing to the tune of whatever music played from her headphones. He spared her only a cursory glance before stalking down the short hallway behind her desk.

"Hey! Can I help you?" she called after him.

Without breaking stride, Cam waved the paper fisted in his hand in her general direction. "I'll help myself."

There were only two doors in the hallway. He stopped in front of the one that sported a brass plate engraved with the words *Madison Daniels, president.*

"You can't just, like, walk in there," the receptionist hollered from behind him. "You've got to, you know, make an appointment if you want to see Miss Daniels."

"Miss," he repeated half to himself. "Of course she's a miss."

The dating service's president was probably some dried-up old prune of a woman whose only enjoyment came from poking her nose into other people's business. "She'll see me now," he said, and pushed open the door.

Inside, the room's lone occupant stood with her back to him looking out the window, which offered a rather uninspiring view of the parking lot. It was late June and already pushing eighty degrees outside, but her arms were wrapped tightly around her middle as if she were chilled to the bone. She turned when he entered and surprise registered on the pale oval of her face.

Cam had to admit, he was surprised, too. This was not the meddling old maid he'd been expecting. Madison Daniels was a looker, with hair as dark and wavy as a gypsy's and an interesting little mole that transformed one eyebrow into a sideways semicolon. The wild mane and sexy mole, however, seemed at odds with the rest of the package. The large eyes that dominated her face were as blue as a summer sky and unmistakably sad. The delicate skin below them looked slightly shadowed, as if she hadn't slept well the night before. Beneath her conservative long-sleeved blouse and tailored navy slacks, her curves were more lean than lush. He pegged her to be in her mid-twenties, about five-five, and maybe one hundred and twenty pounds soaking wet. Fragile. That was the word that came to mind. Her skin was as fair and freckleless as his was tanned. Clearly, she didn't spend much time outdoors, despite the miles of beaches and hiking trails that enticed summer vacationers to the northern Michigan town of Traverse City from near and far. Cam thought he could pity her for that alone.

But pity wasn't why he had come.

"I'd like a word with you."

He watched surprise recede behind a mask of polite, if cool, professionalism, and for some reason he found himself wondering if those full lips of hers remembered how to smile. Yet there was a ghost of humor in her words when she replied, "You look like a man who has more than one word on his mind."

The receptionist huffed into the room then, shooting Cam a nasty look and cracking her gum for good measure.

"Sorry, Miss Daniels. I told this guy he needed an appointment, but he wouldn't listen. He just walked right past me."

"That's all right, Lisa." She sent the young woman a reassuring wink that caused the mole to dip briefly. "I've got nothing pressing at the moment." Glancing in his direction, she asked, "Can I offer you some coffee, Mr....ah, I don't believe I know your name."

"Foley, Cameron Foley," he answered. Her voice was slow and smoky and made him think of the South. Wherever she hailed from originally, it wasn't the Great Lakes state. "And I'll pass on the coffee."

"Very well. Hold my calls, please," she told Lisa,

dismissing her. The receptionist sent Cam one last squinty-eyed glare before closing the door on her way out.

Madison Daniels walked to the high-backed chair behind her desk, her movements stiff, awkward. She sank slowly onto the upholstered seat and folded her hands on the leather blotter. For the first time, Cam noticed the raised scars that ran along the back of her right hand and disappeared beneath the cuff of the long-sleeved blouse. He realized he must have been staring when she discreetly lowered her hands to her lap, away from his prying view.

"Are you interested in signing up for our services, Mr. Foley? We haven't been in business long, but True Love, Incorporated has enjoyed quite a bit of success so far." She plucked a square of ivory vellum from the desk blotter. "In fact, I've just been invited to a wedding."

The woman's fragility momentarily had taken the edge off his anger, but it throbbed back to life now and made him lash out.

"I'm here because of this." He tossed the wadded letter onto her desktop and folded his arms over his chest. "I want to know what gives you the right to mail out solicitations like this one."

She smoothed the wrinkles from the paper, eyebrows tugging together as she read it. Then she glanced up.

"I'm afraid I don't understand, Mr. Foley. This is a simple promotion. Hundreds of other businesses use such mailings. It's all on the up and up, I assure you. We get the names, addresses and marital status from the Secretary of State's office in Lansing. The people who are interested can respond. Those who aren't can toss it in the garbage.''

''No harm, no foul,'' he scoffed. ''Did it ever occur to you that not everyone is single by choice?''

She eyed him warily but nodded in agreement. ''That's precisely why we're in business, to help people who don't want to be single find someone to spend time with—perhaps even a lifetime.''

Cam snorted, irritated anew by her calm demeanor and the slightly sanctimonious edge to her tone.

''Lady, don't pretend your motives are so pure. You're not as interested in helping lonely people find one another as you are in drawing a paycheck.''

She shrugged off the barb, although he thought he saw temper spark briefly in the otherwise calm blue of her eyes.

''Are you lonely, Mr. Foley?''

The way she said it, she reminded Cam of the therapist he'd seen briefly a few summers earlier just after his wife died. He glanced down at the ring on his left hand, the feel of it comforting and familiar. Safe. Just that morning he'd taken it off and tucked it away in the back of his bureau drawer. It was the first time the ring had left his finger in ten years. Everyone kept telling him it was time to move on with his life. They all offered the pathetically clichéd reason that it was what Angela would have wanted—for him and for the daughter they'd made together. It didn't matter that it was true, and that before her death Angela had made him promise to keep his heart open to love and the possibility of remarriage.

Even Angela's own sister, whose grief came the closest to matching his own, was urging him to start dating again. For the past few weeks, he'd actually begun to consider it. Maybe they were right. Maybe it was time to dip his toe in the water again, enjoy some adult company. There were times when he felt so lonely. But then the mail had come that morning, and with it True Love, Incorporated's galling solicitation. How dare they call him single? His hand, wedding ring securely back in place, curled into a fist as outrage returned, fueled by something he refused to admit might be guilt.

"I'm not lonely," he replied between gritted teeth, even though he knew it was a lie.

"But you are single, correct?" She waved a hand toward the solicitation on her desk.

He didn't answer. To say yes seemed a betrayal of Angela, and yet no wasn't quite accurate, either. She apparently took his silence for an affirmation.

"Well, if you're single, I fail to see what the problem is. If you're not interested in our services, fine. Throw the solicitation away. But True Love, Incorporated is doing nothing wrong—morally or legally— by seeking your business. You, Mr. Foley, are the single man living at 4255 Mockingbird Lane to whom this correspondence is addressed."

"No, *Miss* Daniels, I'm not." He laid the palms of his hands on the highly polished wood of her desktop and leaned forward, pinning her with an icy glare that he was gratified to see had her shifting back in her seat.

"What I am is the *widowed* man living at 4255

Mockingbird Lane who watched his wife die a slow
and agonizing death from cancer. What I am, *Miss*
Daniels, is a man who wants to be left the hell alone
by people like you who have the audacity to try to
put a price tag on something that's beyond monetary
value.

"True Love, Incorporated." He sneered. "You
ought to be arrested for fraud. You don't know the
first thing about true love. If you did, you'd realize it
can't be packaged and sold like cereal in some gro-
cery store."

Her face bleached of what little color it had. In a
shaky whisper, she replied, "I'm so sorry. H-how
long ago did you lose your wife?"

He backed up a step, crossed his arms again. "It
was three years in May."

"That's a long time."

"It's an eternity."

"Have...have you dated at all since then?"

He glared at her and said with a certainty he did
not feel, "I have no reason to date. There's no one
I'd be interested in meeting."

"How can you be so sure?"

How? He twirled the band that encircled the third
finger with the thumb of his left hand. The gesture
was comforting, familiar, affirming.

"I've already had my 'true love,' Miss Daniels.
There's not another one out there."

Despite his intentionally surly tone, the woman
faced him calmly, reminding him again of that loathe-
some therapist his sister-in-law had badgered him into
seeing.

"I've read that those who love deeply once are more likely to love deeply again. Who's to say there's not someone else who could make you happy? You're a young man, Mr. Foley. Surely you don't plan to spend the rest of your life alone?"

Young or not, that's precisely what he planned—until just recently. Guilt nipped him again. "Let me guess. You think you can help me find the perfect woman."

"That *is* my business." One finely arched eyebrow lifted, tugging that intriguing little mole along with it. "Care to let me try?"

"No."

"Why not? If you don't believe in my service, what do you have to worry about?"

It wasn't quite a dare, but it seemed awfully close. He narrowed his eyes. "What's in it for you?"

"Nothing, really. I'll even waive my usual fee. Call it a goodwill gesture."

Good will, my butt, Cam thought. But two could play her game, and he was curious just how far she would go with her little matchmaking scheme. Make the stakes high enough, and she would back down.

"All right," he said slowly, stalling so he could think. "But let's sweeten the pot with a deadline. Forget true love, I'll give you until…Valentine's Day to find me a woman worth a second date. If you succeed, I'll pay you twice your normal fee. Heck, I'll even do a testimonial if you want."

"And if I fail?"

She wasn't backing down, he realized. Time to tighten the screws. Cam leaned forward, offered his most carnivorous smile. "If you fail, you'll take out a full-page ad in the *Traverse City Record-Eagle* admitting you're a lousy matchmaker, admitting, *Miss* Daniels, that you are a fraud."

That should do it, he thought, as he watched her eyelids flicker in shock.

"That would destroy my business."

"If you believe in your service, what do you have to worry about?" he said, parroting her earlier comment.

Her lips thinned, settling into a tight line. He knew he had her. She wouldn't agree, which suited him fine. He had no desire to be fixed up with strange and probably desperate women. Feeling magnanimous, he decided a heartfelt apology on her part would suffice. As well as a solemn promise to take his name off her business's mailing list.

But then she stuck out her scarred right hand.

"You have a deal, Mr. Foley."

Maddie rather liked the way her announcement caused Cameron Foley's mouth to slacken in surprise. Opened or closed, it was a nice mouth, the bottom lip slightly fuller than the top one. But there was nothing soft about his features, nothing that could be called feminine. Cameron Foley was all man, from the slight stubble that shaded his strong jaw to the clearly defined muscles of his forearms. He reminded her a little of the actor Dennis Quaid, ruggedly masculine, cocky, just a bit reckless. And incredibly sexy. The unexpected direction of her thoughts shocked Maddie. In her line of work, of course she noticed such details about men. But this wasn't some mere clinical observation—the little tug of attraction was as unmistakable as it was unwelcome and pointless. She lowered the hand that he had yet to shake and fiddled with a paper clip while she waited for him to find his voice.

Finally, he said hoarsely, "I do?"

To lighten her own mood she quipped, "Practicing for the wedding already?"

"Let's get one thing straight," he bit out, his face darkening like a thundercloud. "I'm not looking for another wife. No one can replace Angela."

"Please forgive me. I was only teasing, but it was in extremely poor taste. You're right. No one will ever hold that same place in your heart." Her tone earnest, she continued, "But perhaps I can introduce you to someone whose company you'll enjoy. Someone you'll want to take out on that second date. So, do we still have a deal?"

Maddie wasn't sure why she felt so compelled to help him. She had far more to lose than he did. But something about Cameron Foley tugged at her, making her want to reach out. Perhaps it was because despite all of his angry denials, he seemed so lonely.

He hesitated a moment, looking torn, before giving a jerky nod. And Maddie got the feeling that even though he'd been the one to set the terms, his participation in their wager would be begrudging at best. Well, the race went to the swift, so Maddie pulled her chair closer to the desk and booted up the computer.

"Terrific. I'll need to gather some background information. Standard stuff like date of birth, height, weight, health history, that kind of thing. If you'll take a seat we can get started."

He backed up a step. "I don't have time for that today. Driving into the city for this little discussion has put me behind schedule as it is. Some of us have *real* work to do."

Ignoring the insult, she said, "Tomorrow, then?"

"Busy. Sorry." He tucked his hands in the front pockets of a pair of well-worn jeans, looking not the least bit contrite.

The chair's upholstery creaked as Maddie leaned forward and rested her elbows on the desk. "Do you plan to win this bet by default, Mr. Foley? I realize Valentine's Day is nearly eight months away, but that's not a lot of time. It will be a few weeks before I even have your video and background ready."

"No video."

"No video," she repeated, and blew out a sigh of frustration. "So, you want to see them, but they can't see you, is that the idea?"

"I don't need to see them." He inclined his head, smiled mockingly. "If you're as good as you say you are, *Miss* Daniels, I'd be a fool not to trust your expert judgment. Besides, this way you can't claim afterward that I only picked women I knew wouldn't suit me."

"Oh, I'm good," she assured him, and had to quash the urge to blush when one of his eyebrows inched up in unmistakable male speculation. It didn't seem to matter that she knew he was deliberately baiting her.

"Of course, I'll have to do a more thorough screening than usual, which means taking up more of your time," she said as sweetly as possible. "I'll need to know everything about you, Mr. Foley, your likes, dislikes—all the telling little quirks and habits that often come through in my clients' videos. So, when do we start?''

A muscle jumped in his jaw as he pulled his hands from his pockets and settled them on his hips. He glanced away, and she thought he might be ready to renege on the hasty bargain they'd struck. But then his gaze drifted back to hers and his lips twitched with a smirk.

''When you buy that ad in the *Record-Eagle*, I want it to be in color. It'll attract more attention that way—and it will be more expensive.''

She fought the urge to roll her eyes. Such a reaction would be neither professional nor, as her mother would point out if present, ladylike. Still, she made a mental note to write in Cameron Foley's file that the man could be insufferable when he thought he was on the winning side of an argument.

''Fine, but it won't come to that.'' An idea occurred to her then. ''I have a little stipulation of my own.''

''And that is?''

''The second date, you'll bring roses—a dozen, long-stemmed and red. And you'll take her to the Trillium,'' Maddie added, naming one of the area's nicest and priciest restaurants. ''You do own a suit, I hope, because you'll have to wear one.''

She pretended not to hear him mutter something obscene about neckties.

''So, when do we get started?'' she asked again.

''Thursday is the best I can do, say noon, and you'll have to come to me.'' He nodded toward the wrinkled paper on her desk. "You know where I live."

He walked to the door and opened it, but hesitated at the threshold. Turning, he smiled, losing all semblance of the outraged man whose grief had propelled him to stomp into her office fifteen minutes earlier, demanding an explanation, expecting an apology. But, if possible, his calm demeanor and that devilishly sexy grin on his face made Maddie even more determined.

"I'm going to win," he said with conviction.

"Yes, Mr. Foley, you are." She allowed herself a moment to enjoy his startled expression, before adding, "Just not the way you think."

It was dark when Maddie arrived at her apartment, the converted upstairs of a souvenir shop in Traverse City's quaint downtown. The shop had long since closed for the day, but several nearby restaurants and bars were open, so the streets were cluttered with tourists—"fudgies" as the locals liked to call them. The term was both derogatory and affectionate. The area's economy—including its fudge shops—largely depended on down-staters, but no one particularly cared for the staggering crush of humanity that invaded the northern Michigan town almost as soon as the ice melted on the bay.

Maddie had no view of Lake Michigan's lovely aqua water from her tiny living room window, and a closet might have been more spacious than the place's only bedroom. It was a definite step down from the comfortable house she'd grown up in, and a huge tumble from the large Grosse Pointe estate she'd last called home. Its main selling points were cheap rent and a central location. She could walk to work—a definite plus since she didn't care to drive even though she had a car, and the exercise was good physical therapy.

She toed off her flats, leaving them on the mat by the front door. A lamp burned cheerfully in her living room thanks to a timer, but other than that the place was dark and quiet. Lonely quiet, which was why she preferred to work late. No reason to rush home to an empty apartment. An empty life.

As she crossed the room to draw the blinds, she glanced hopefully at the answering machine. No messages. She picked up the phone, dialed the familiar number and waited. Her mother answered on the fourth ring, the South thick in Eliza Daniels's honeyed tone.

"Hello, Mother. It's Maddie."

"Why, Madison, this is a surprise. It's rather late. Your father and I were just getting ready for bed. How are you, dear?"

"I'm fine." The polite response slipped effortlessly from Maddie's lips. She shook her head, tried again with the truth. "Actually, Mother, I'm not fine. In fact, I'm having a really bad day."

On the other end of the line, Eliza made an appropriately sympathetic sound. "I'm sorry to hear that you're under the weather. Is it your…*infirmity* that's giving you trouble?"

If it hadn't so perfectly summed up the awkwardness of their relationship, Maddie might have chuckled at the discreet euphemism and the way her mother's tone grew hushed whenever she used it.

"I am a bit sore today, but that's not what's bothering me. Do...do you know what today is?"

"Today? Hmm. I'm afraid not."

For some reason—call it blind hope—Maddie had expected her mother, of all people, to know, to remember.

"Today should have been Michael's birthday."

"Michael's birthday?"

"If he'd been born on his due date, he would have turned one...today."

Maddie had spent her lunch hour beside his small gravesite—a gravesite only she had ever visited. Silence greeted her stifled sob, and she kicked herself mentally for seeking comfort and commiseration where neither had been forthcoming in the past.

"A good night's sleep is what you need, dear. You'll feel better in the morning."

"My baby will still be dead in the morning. No amount of sleep is going to change that. Why can't we ever talk about what happened, Mother?" she beseeched.

Eliza Daniels considered an emotional outburst as gauche as wearing white shoes after Labor Day. It simply was not done. She went on as if Maddie had not spoken. "Do you have any of those pills left that the doctor prescribed after the accident? Perhaps you should take one."

Ah, yes, as far as her mother was concerned, there was nothing a little Valium couldn't fix. Maddie shook her head in sad acceptance. Arguing would be pointless. "Yes, perhaps I'll do that. I should have thought of it myself. Thank you, Mother."

Relief evident in her tone, Eliza replied, "You're welcome, dear. Sleep well."

"I'm sure I will. Give Daddy my love."

Maddie hung up, feeling even more fatigued. Her limp was more pronounced as she trudged down the short hall to the bathroom and turned on the tub's faucet. She wouldn't resort to a tranquilizer, but a nice long soak might ease the aching pain in her knee and hip. She added a capful of lavender-scented bubble bath.

She shed her clothing, secured her hair in a quick topknot, and gingerly lowered her scarred body into the bathwater. As it had for the past several months, work remained her best source of escape, so she redirected her thoughts to Cameron Foley and the unconventional bargain they'd struck earlier in the day. He said he wanted to be left alone, but despite his vehement words, Maddie hadn't been convinced. It was the aching loss evident beneath his gruff words that had prompted her to put her livelihood on the line to find him a match. He seemed so in need of a happy ending.

"A happy ending," she mused aloud. The words echoed in the tiny bathroom, taunting her.

Cameron Foley had accused Maddie of being a fraud, and perhaps she was. At the very least, she knew she was guilty of living vicariously. There would be no happy ending for her.

She glanced at her left hand, which was ringless now. The sad truth was that as hard as she worked to find matches and mates for her clients, at twenty-eight, Maddie Daniels was divorced, broken and alone. And she had long since given up any hope of knowing or deserving the kind of true love that caused Cameron Foley to still mourn a wife who'd been dead three years.

Chapter Two

Thursday dawned clear and bright, the perfect weather for a drive. The roads were dry, the sun a warm, glowing orb climbing higher in the eastern sky. Even so, Maddie's footsteps were hesitant as she walked to the parking lot behind the souvenir shop. Her slow pace had nothing to do with the stiffness in her leg and hip. In addition to her trepidation about seeing Cameron Foley again, she hated to drive.

Biting her lip, she slid onto the front seat of her car and fastened the safety belt even before inserting the key into the ignition. Since the accident fifteen months earlier, she'd gotten past the paralyzing fear of being in an automobile, but not the passionate dislike of operating one.

Driving five miles under the posted speed limit, she pulled onto Highway 22 and headed north toward the tiny, artsy town of Suttons Bay. To her right, sunlight danced on the calm waters of the west arm of Grand

Traverse Bay. To her left, vacation homes dotted the hillside. The farther she drove, however, the more rural the landscape became. She smiled as row after row of cherry trees replaced man-made structures on the rolling countryside. The trees were heavy with fruit now, their boughs seeming to bend under the weight of sweet cherries that already looked ripe and inviting. This was cherry country, and despite the constant development pressure farmers felt to sell off the prime land their orchards occupied, the local people were proud of their crop. Eighty percent of the nation's cherries were grown here and in a handful of other Michigan counties.

Recalling the statistic, Maddie wasn't surprised when five miles outside of Suttons Bay, she spotted the big red sign that read Foley Cherry Farm.

"Of course."

She might have guessed Cameron's occupation. His tanned face and forearms, as well as the well-worn denim that had hugged his powerful build, had all hinted at time spent outdoors.

Gravel crunched under her tires when she turned the car onto Mockingbird Lane, nothing but a plume of dust visible through her rearview mirror. It had been a dry spring, and summer wasn't promising to be any wetter. Cherry trees lined either side of the road as far as she could see, lush with fruit and postcard perfect. Finally, a large farmhouse came into view. It was set back from the road on the crest of a hill, its lowest level partially built into the slope. A big bay window jutted from the stone facade, above it two cedar-shingled gables gazed cheerfully out over the orchards.

It was a beautiful home, a serene setting, but Maddie's pulse throbbed in her temples as she parked the car and gathered her briefcase. *What kind of mood would Cameron Foley be in today?*

Shrugging off her nerves, she walked to the front door. It was yanked open before she could knock. A girl of about six stood in front of her. She wore denim overall shorts and a pink shirt. Her dark hair was pulled into a pair of adorably crooked pigtails. There were matching bandages on her knees and a smudge of something that looked like flour on one of her chubby cheeks.

She eyed Maddie speculatively before asking, "Who are you?" The words whistled out from the darling gap between her two front teeth.

Maddie leaned forward at the waist. When she was nearly eye level with the girl, she replied, "I'm Maddie Daniels. And who might you be?"

"I'm Caroline Foley. I live here."

"You're lucky. It's a nice house."

The girl shrugged, then her pixie face scrunched comically. "Are you the know-it-all I heard Daddy telling Mrs. Haversham about?"

The insult, delivered so earnestly in the child's squeaky voice, caused Maddie to chuckle. "Yes, that would be me."

So, Cameron Foley had a daughter, a delightful little imp of a girl who apparently had inherited her father's gift for being blunt. The envy she felt was instantaneous and accompanied by a painful mental chorus of "if onlys."

"Oh, Miss Daniels!" a woman called, rushing into the foyer behind Caroline. She was about sixty and as plump as a Thanksgiving turkey. "I'm Mrs. Haversham, Cam's housekeeper. He told me to expect you."

Maddie shook off her melancholy and sent Caroline a wink as she straightened. "So I hear. And call me Maddie, please."

"It's nice to meet you, Maddie." Mrs. Haversham wiped a pair of thick hands on the apron she wore and glanced over her shoulder when a timer chimed.

"I hope I haven't come at a bad time. Mr. Foley did tell me noon."

"Not at all. That will be my apple pie. Cam is in the orchard. He said to send you out when you got here." She turned to Caroline, surreptitiously wiping the flour from the little girl's cheek with a grandmotherly pat. "Dearie, why don't you show Maddie the way?"

Maddie followed Caroline around the side of the house, across the lawn and into the orchard, falling farther behind with each tentative step she took. Walking on a sidewalk often proved a trial, but walking on an uneven dirt path littered with nature's debris had Maddie wishing she'd brought the cane she'd relegated to the back of her closet. She hated the thing and the way it advertised her disability, but using it would have been far less humiliating than what happened to her next. She stumbled, her foot twisting on an exposed root, and her world tilted. Windmilling her arms like something out of a Saturday morning cartoon did nothing to restore her precarious balance, but it did send her briefcase flying. To her utter mortification, Maddie landed with a jarring thud on her backside in the middle of Cameron Foley's orchard.

"Caroline!" she called. The little girl had danced several yards ahead, propelled by the boundless energy of youth, but she bulleted back now, eyes huge at the sight of an adult sprawled on the ground.

"Gosh, are you hurt?"

"No." Unless she counted her pride, Maddie thought wryly. "But I think I'll just rest for a moment. Could you, um, go find your father and ask him to meet me here?"

Maddie watched Caroline shoot down a row of trees, envying the girl's surefootedness. When she was alone, she put dignity aside and crawled on all fours to the briefcase and the smattering of papers that had tumbled out of its exterior pockets. She gathered them up, stuffed them back in and was preparing to use the case as leverage to help her stand when an incredulous deep voice stopped her cold.

"What the heck happened to you?"

Cameron Foley could hardly believe his eyes. Maddie Daniels was kneeling in the dirt. The woman had fallen, just as his daughter had claimed when she'd come tearing down one of the rows of tart cherries he'd been walking along with a worker. Cam almost smiled at the picture the woman presented. Dust covered her navy slacks and a wave of dark hair dangled in front of her eyes. He never would have taken the cool, competent Miss Daniels for such a klutz.

"She fell, Daddy. I told you," Caroline chirped, clearly perplexed by her father's short memory.

"I see that, honey. Now, why don't you run back to the house and tell Mrs. Haversham to put on a fresh pot of coffee. We'll be along shortly."

When his daughter was out of hearing range, he said, "I hope you're not going to sue me. I'd hate to have to turn my farm into a condo development to pay out a personal injury settlement to some clumsy female."

"Your concern is truly enough to make me weep," Maddie replied, her tone as dry as the dusty patch of earth beneath her knees. Cam gave her points for dignity. Her stiff upper lip appeared unaffected, which probably was more than could be said for her dust-covered derriere.

"Yeah, well, why don't we head back to the house? Less chance for you to get hurt sitting in my kitchen. I hope."

It was a cheap shot, but he wasn't feeling particularly cordial at the moment. He didn't have time for this today. He didn't have time for *her* any day. How he wished he'd never let pride push him into this foolish bargain.

He glanced around the orchard and suppressed the urge to sigh. It was not quite July, but a warm spring had caused the cherries to ripen early. The sweets were almost two weeks ahead of schedule, and the tarts were right behind them. If some of the trees weren't shaken soon the fruit would spoil. He'd lost some of his help to better-paying jobs, three of his best workers in the past month alone. The good economy made it hard to keep employees, especially when the same economy didn't do much for the price that cherries brought at market.

"We'll have to make this quick. Daylight is dollars to a farmer, Miss Daniels." He snatched up the briefcase and started off for the house.

"Mr. Foley."

She brought him up short when she called his name in that formal, Southern-sounding way of hers.

What now? He blew out an exasperated breath before turning around, but the pithy comment he planned died on his lips when he realized she had not moved. She was still on the ground, one leg pulled beneath her as if she had tried to stand. The other one, however, was bent at a rather awkward angle out to the side.

"I'm afraid I can't get up on my own." The words were issued in a stilted whisper and her gaze slid away as she said them. A blush the color of ripe tart cherries darkened her fair cheeks.

Still not looking directly at him, she extended the scarred hand and Cam's memory stirred. That day in her office her movements had seemed stiff and hesitant, painful even. Clearly, whatever accident had left her hand so marred had done far more serious damage to her leg. *And he'd left her sitting in the dirt.* He closed his eyes briefly, ashamed that his rude behavior had forced her to all but beg for his help.

Cam clasped the hand Maddie held out and, as gently as possible, helped her to her feet, apologizing profusely as he did so.

"You know, I'm not usually such a jerk."

She was gracious enough to let him off the hook easily. "It's all right, really." She reached for the briefcase he still held.

"I'll carry it for you. Is your leg…how did…?" He let the questions trail away on a hastily expelled breath. "Sorry. It's really none of my business."

She answered him, anyway, unintentionally creating more questions with her vague explanation. "I was in an accident. Sometimes it's hard to get up."

"Are you sure you're okay?"

"Relax, Mr. Foley. I won't be suing you, if that's what's got you worried."

Cam winced. "I was only joking when I said that."

"Really? And here I was already picking out colors for my condominium." She brushed the dust from her clothes, and, inclining her head in the direction of the house, she said, "Shall we?"

Cam walked slowly this time, moderating his usually brisk stride to match her more halting one. It seemed to take forever to reach the house on their silent, slow walk back, giving him plenty of time to feel like a proper heel. They entered through a screened-in back porch, and the homey scents of apples and cinnamon greeted them.

"Mmm. It smells wonderful in here," Maddie said.

"Mrs. Haversham promised Caroline apple pie for dessert. In the three years she's worked for me, she's never broken a promise to my daughter. I make sure her paycheck reflects my appreciation." He motioned toward the table. "Why don't we have a seat in here?"

Gratefully, he noticed his housekeeper and daughter were nowhere to be found, and hopefully they would stay that way for the duration of his interview with Maddie. As it was, Mrs. H. was already too eager for him to start dating again, and who knew what embarrassing things Caroline would blurt out. She was six, after all. That made her old enough to express her thoughts clearly and too young to censor the more inappropriate ones.

"I see the coffee is ready. Would you care for a cup?"

"Please. I take it black. Before we get started, is there someplace I could freshen up?"

"Just down that hallway on the left." Despite her composed demeanor, Cam could almost feel her discomfort.

While he waited for her to return, he poured them both a steaming mug of coffee, lacing his own with a spoonful of sugar. When she reentered the kitchen, the last physical traces of her ordeal in the orchard had been wiped away.

"I'll try to take up as little of your time as possible," she said, slowly lowering herself onto the chair across from him. "I'll need a photograph, just for my records, really. I brought my Polaroid."

She pulled it from the interior of her briefcase, and before he had a chance to protest, she snapped his picture. While she waited for the image to develop, she surprised him by slipping a pair of glasses onto the slim bridge of her nose. They should have made her look even more professional, but Cam had long considered glasses scholarly and...sexy. He chased the thought away with a gulp of coffee, scalding his tongue in the process. Maddie glanced up in question when he hissed out a breath.

"Ready when you are," he managed to say.

"Why don't we start with the basics? Age?"

"Thirty-six. I'll be thirty-seven in March."

She wrote his response on a yellow legal pad. Other notes had already been jotted down in her no-nonsense script. He couldn't quite make out the words, which were upside-down from his vantage point, but he thought he caught something about "well built and attractive." He felt his face heat.

"Height?"

"Just a hair over six feet." For some reason, he straightened in his chair as he said it.

"Weight?"

Cam sipped his coffee, blowing on it beforehand this time, and thought about what the scale had said just that morning. "Um, one-eighty."

She glanced up. One eyebrow lifted over the top rim of her glasses, leaving that little mole hidden.

"Give or take a few," he amended. "Caroline has been on a pizza kick lately and it's easier to cave in than to argue with her." When Maddie just kept staring at him, he added, "She's six, but she's good."

One-eighty, give or take a few pounds, Maddie mused, and probably all muscle. As interesting as she found it that a man would hedge about his weight, she was more intrigued by the way this man looked. A faded Cherry Republic T-shirt stretched over his broad shoulders, and she recalled that softly molded denim had hugged a pair of well-formed thighs when he'd walked.

She cleared her throat, perplexed by the inappropriate direction her thoughts kept taking. Her voice was an embarrassing squeak when she asked her next pitifully obvious question.

"Occupation?"

"I'm a cherry farmer, Miss Daniels." He grinned, a flash of white teeth in an otherwise bronze face, and nodded toward the window and the start of the orchard visible through it. "Foleys have farmed this land for three generations. My dad met my mother here. She was a migrant worker, one of the thousands of Mexicans who came to Michigan each summer to harvest the cherries before modern technology made hand-picking obsolete."

Maddie studied his features. His hair was a light, sun-kissed brown, but the warm hue of his skin and the coffee-colored eyes that peered at her from below a slash of dark brows hinted at his heritage.

She broke off her gaze and pretended to jot down more notes.

"Do you smoke?"

"No, filthy habit."

She stifled a relieved sigh. She couldn't agree more. Of course, she told herself that the relief she felt was merely because finding Cameron Foley a match would be that much easier if he didn't have a pack-a-day habit. The vast majority of her clients were nonsmokers.

"Do you drink?"

"I like a cold beer after a hard day."

That fit, she thought, working up the mental image. She could picture him hoisting a long-necked brown bottle in the evenings, sitting on the steps of that inviting front porch, maybe listening to Ernie Harwell call a Tigers game on the radio.

Then he threw her a curve.

"And I like wine. I sometimes have a glass with dinner. I'm not particularly a connoisseur," he admitted with a shrug. "But I'm partial to anything French and expensive."

"French and expensive," she repeated. This new data did not compute.

"Sure. No one knows grapes like the French. But, I have to say, the local vineyards are coming along. In fact, a few of the Leelanau wines are passably good. Have you tried any?"

"No, I'm afraid I don't get out much," she said as she wrote down *social drinker*.

Cam frowned. "You don't get out much? That seems kind of odd for the president of a dating service."

"My business is relatively young, so I spend most of my days, including weekends, at the office. It doesn't leave a lot of time for anything else."

The explanation seemed perfectly logical. Cam knew all about the demands of being the boss, meeting a payroll while trying to turn a profit, but for some reason he didn't buy it. A woman with her looks would attract plenty of male attention. So why would she choose to spend Saturday nights alone?

Maddie settled the glasses more firmly on the bridge of her nose and said, "Let's move on to your health. Is there anything, ah, contagious that I should know about? Anything you're being treated for?"

The tone was polite enough to make him smile, especially since she was essentially asking him if he had a social disease. Again, he caught the slight hint of the South in her speech.

"You're not from around here, are you? Originally, I mean?"

"No."

"Your accent, I'm guessing South Carolina."

"Georgia, actually. I grew up just outside Atlanta. My parents and brothers still live there."

"Really? Kind of chilly up here for a Southern belle, especially come January. That's one of the reasons my parents moved to Florida when they retired five years ago. What made you decide to relocate to northern Michigan?"

Before she could respond, he grinned and added, "I'm guessing it was a man, and I'm guessing it was a while ago. You've lost a lot of your honeyed drawl, Miss Daniels."

Maddie didn't like the way he'd taken over the interview or the way he had begun to probe into her personal life. He was good at it, too. She *had* moved north to be with a man—the man who, as of nine months ago, had become her ex-husband.

Turning her tone to one of frosted efficiency, she said, "That's not really important. The point of this interview is for me to gather enough information to put together a basic personality sketch of you. I know your time is valuable, so, if you don't mind, I'll ask the questions. Health?" she repeated.

His lips thinned into a serious line, and he answered rather pointedly, "My health is excellent. I've been out of circulation too long to have caught any-thing deadly.''

She bobbled the coffee she'd been about to sip, although she managed not to spill any of it on her blouse. ''What kind of woman would you say you prefer?''

It was his turn to be uncomfortable. He straightened in his seat and twirled the spoon in the sugar bowl. ''I don't know. I'm not very particular.''

Hogwash, Maddie thought. Cameron Foley would be *very* particular. Any man who would drive into Traverse City during the height of tourist season to protest a dating service's mass mailing clearly had an opinion on more than mere marketing practices.

''I can't do my job if you're not candid. We had a deal, Mr. Foley.''

''Cameron,'' he corrected her, sounding slightly ir-ritated. ''My friends call me Cam. Since you're dig-ging into my personal life, I'm thinking you should at least call me by my given name.''

''Very well.'' She took a deep breath and settled on the more formal moniker. ''Cameron.'' The word seemed to linger on her tongue like peppermint candy.

''Does this mean I can call you Madison?'' She thought he might be teasing her. A light danced in his dark eyes, but his lips remained unbowed.

''Maddie, please. Only my mother calls me Madi-son. And my father, when I've tried his patience.''

''I'll bet that's often,'' he muttered.

''Excuse me?''

''Nothing. Isn't Madison an odd name for a girl?''

His gaze skimmed down her torso, lingered an uncomfortable moment. "Woman," he corrected himself.

She felt herself blush. "My father is an American history buff. He's big on presidents. I have two brothers, Lincoln and Carter."

"A Republican and a Democrat. At least your father is bipartisan."

She couldn't quite stifle the unladylike snort of laughter that would have earned her mother's censure. "My father's a dyed-in-the-wool Democrat. That's why he named my mother's cat Nixon. Cats are too brazen and calculating to be named after Democrats, he claims."

"Clearly this was before the Clinton administration," Cam muttered.

She cleared her throat. "While I find your political views fascinating, I think we should get back to your preferences in women. Do you prefer blondes?"

Some men did, Cam thought, but not him. He'd never found a blonde to be half as sexy as a brunette. Perhaps that was part of his heritage poking through. He glanced at Maddie's dark cascade of loose curls. The sunlight filtering through the window exposed its burnished highlights. Angela's hair had been like that, dark and yet full of secrets that could be teased out by the sun. He'd loved to touch her hair, to bury his fingers in it. The memory made him ache.

"Blondes," he blurted out. Trying to sound less defensive he added, "Yeah, I prefer blondes."

"Tall, petite, slim, um...well-proportioned?"

He noted her discomfort, and the devil made him

say, "I like tall women. And I like them to have a little meat on their bones. A little more meat in some places than others, if you know what I mean."

She scribbled something on the notepad and, without looking up, she asked, "Any other physical attributes you find appealing, Mr., um, Cameron?"

"Legs. Long legs with thin ankles. Oh, and small feet. Nothing over size seven."

He thought she might have rolled her eyes, but she kept her head slightly bent as she continued, "Do you have an age range that you would prefer?"

He didn't really care about age. Angie had been a year older than he. But he stroked his chin, as if considering. "Hmm, how old are you?"

Maddie appeared startled. "Me?"

"Yeah, you."

She tucked a lush wave of hair behind her ear. It was one of the few utterly female things he'd seen her do, and he found it intriguing. Almost as intriguing as the way that little mole dipped and lifted with her every expression.

"Twenty-eight." She tucked more hair behind her other ear and moistened her lips before adding, "Last month."

She looked younger than that right now, despite the eyewear and the formal air she put on.

"Ah, well, you'd be a little old for me, then. I think I'd prefer a woman in her early twenties at this point in my life," Cam replied.

She definitely rolled her eyes at that, although she tried to hide it by pushing up her glasses. But her tone remained professional and impassive when she continued with, "Do you have a problem with a woman who was married and is either divorced or widowed now?"

"No divorcées."

Maddie stopped writing and hugged the yellow pad of paper to her chest. The pose struck him as oddly defensive.

"Why's that?"

"I took those same vows, and I made them work. Even when Angela got sick. Even when it got really ugly. 'Til death do us part.' I'm not interested in someone who can't keep their end of the bargain."

Her expression remained clouded, but she nodded. "I can understand that."

"Good, because I won't compromise on this point."

It was just icing on the cake if his stand on principle made it that much harder for her to fix him up. He wondered if that was why she seemed to take it so personally.

"Very well. What about…children? What if the woman either never married or is widowed and has children?"

He slouched back in his chair and folded his arms, the memories swarming him like flies at a barbecue. When he finally spoke, the words seemed to scrape against his throat, leaving it raw and aching.

"I like kids. Angie and I planned to have a big family, perhaps because each of us came from such small families. I'm an only child and Angie has one sister. Caroline was just starting to crawl when Ang first got sick." He swallowed thickly, but the bitterness and something even more acidic remained. He doubted he would ever forget the terrible panic he'd experienced the day he first heard a doctor say the word *cancer*.

"So, you don't mind children," Maddie prodded, her tone gentle and magnolia-kissed.

"No. I like kids. One of my biggest regrets is that we weren't able to have more before...I guess I would just prefer someone who got married *first*."

"Is that another one of the points on which you won't compromise?"

"Yes."

She made a final note before sliding the pen behind her ear. Most of the ballpoint was lost immediately in the wavy mass of mahogany. Again, he found himself thinking that there was something out of place about that hair on Maddie Daniels. In every other way she was a polished, buttoned-down professional. Practical and conservative, almost to the point of being prim. She was a woman who wore classic styles that would look as tidy and unobtrusive in ten years as they did today. Yet the hair curled around her face, a little unruly, a tad spirited and free. He wondered if that was intentional or a piece of her subconscious poking through.

"So, just to recap, you're looking for a tall, well-endowed blonde with great legs and small feet who is in her early twenties, never divorced and possibly the mother of children. Does that sound about right?"

It didn't sound right at all, but Cam nodded, anyway. What did it matter? Maddie Daniels could ask all the questions she wanted. She could take all the information she wanted and feed it into some computer database filled with other singles. But she would never be able to find him a perfect match, another true love.

"Give me a couple of weeks to sort through everything. Then I'll give you a call." She stuffed the notepad and pen back into her briefcase and pulled off the glasses before rising.

"I'll look forward to it."

"Yes," she said dryly. "I'm sure you will."

Later that evening, while Maddie nibbled on a turkey sandwich in her quiet apartment, she spread out her notes on the small coffee table in front of the couch and went over Cameron's responses one more time. So much of what he'd said had come as no surprise. Yet Maddie couldn't say why it bothered her so much that his ideal woman seemed to be the antithesis of her: blond, younger, voluptuous, never divorced. She rubbed her aching knee and hip. He wanted a woman with great legs, and he liked children, so it followed that he would want a woman who could have them. The doctors had been clear on that point—Maddie would never become pregnant again.

Well, what did it matter that she wasn't his type? She had no cause to feel slighted, no right to feel sorry for herself that her future yawned long and lonely. Maddie's job was to find matches for her clients, and she was good at it. Very good.

The Polaroid snapshot she'd taken of Cameron was paper-clipped to the outside of a file folder marked with his name. She ran a fingertip over the strong, stubborn line of his jaw.

"I'm going to find someone to make you happy, Cameron Foley," she vowed.

Chapter Three

On Saturday morning, Maddie decided to indulge herself with a rare day off of work. Traverse City's annual weeklong National Cherry Festival was gearing up, and the televised coverage showed that tourists and residents alike were standing five deep along the parade route that snaked through downtown.

Maddie wasn't one for crowds. Just the thought of being jostled and shoved in an exuberant sea of humanity made her eager to stay well out of its range. But the throbbing cadence of the marching bands had her tapping her toes as she sat on the couch reading the newspaper. And the cheerful chatter and excited laughter that floated through her open windows made it seem obscene to stay cooped up in her apartment, watching the parade on her small television, when she could hear it passing a couple of blocks away.

Besides, the day promised to be gorgeous, perfect for spending a little time outdoors, soaking up a ju-

dicious amount of sun while wearing a judicious
amount of sunscreen. She would just walk down to
the small coffee shop on Front Street and grab a cup
of the house blend, staying as far away from the
crowds as possible and experiencing the excitement
of the parade from the periphery. She shrugged off
the uncomfortable thought that too much of her life
seemed to be lived that way these days—on the sidelines, watching rather than participating.

She applied a liberal amount of sunscreen to her
face, neck and forearms, and dressed in a pair of
white cotton slacks and a bright red T-shirt in honor
of the occasion. The shirt had three-quarter-length
sleeves, but it still exposed her right arm from just
below the elbow. She stood in front of the full-length
mirror that hung on the back of the bathroom door
and nibbled her bottom lip. With the fingers of her
left hand, she skimmed the length of the ugly scar. It
had faded some in the months since the accident, but
it was still a hideous purplish red, although the doctors assured her that someday it would turn a less eye-
catching white.

Whether it was mottled red or shiny white, Maddie
would always know it was there. She would always
know the utter failure it represented. She could hide
it from prying eyes with long sleeves, but she couldn't
hide it from herself. So what was the point? Securing
her hair into a ponytail, she went off in search of her
sneakers.

Maddie walked close to the buildings, brushing a
hand along the reassuring comfort of their solid sur-
faces. Well back from the milling crowds, she

couldn't see much of the passing parade, except for the tops of some of the taller floats as they made their way down Front Street and a brightly suited clown who played a tiny concertina as he walked along on stilts. At the coffee shop, she ducked inside, grateful for the short line, but customers filled the small shop's six indoor tables. Cradling the insulated cup in her palm, she returned outside, knowing even before she looked that the half-dozen wrought-iron tables arranged along the sidewalk would be occupied as well. Determined to enjoy the morning sun's warmth on her face, she ignored the ache in her hip, leaned against the building's brick facade and sipped her coffee.

''Maddie!'' a high-pitched voice squealed a moment later.

She glanced to her right in time to see Caroline Foley closing the distance between them at a full-out run. The child's pixie face was smudged with tears. Even more surprising, when Caroline reached Maddie, she barely managed to come to a complete stop before she threw her arms around Maddie's waist in a hug so fierce, it almost knocked them both over. As it was, it succeeded in spilling most of Maddie's coffee on the sidewalk.

''Hey, what's happened?'' she asked, when she'd managed to pry Caroline loose.

The girl's lower lip trembled and a pair of fat tears spilled down her cheeks. ''My daddy got lost.''

''I see.'' Maddie set what was left of her coffee on the ledge of the shop's front window and reached into her pocket for a tissue. Dabbing at the dirty tear tracks on Caroline's face, she asked, "Do you remember where he was before he wandered off?"

A pair of slim shoulders shrugged as Caroline shuddered out a breath. "H-he was talking to Aunt Eve. Uncle Richard and the boys had gone to get elephant ears. I wanted to go, too, but Daddy said I had to wait. Then he just...disappeared."

"I'm glad you saw me," Maddie said, giving Caroline a quick squeeze.

"Should we go look for him? He's probably pretty s-scared." The little girl's lower lip trembled again.

"I'll bet he is," Maddie agreed. "It's pretty scary to be lost, especially in a crowd as big as this. But no, I don't think we should go look for him. I think we should stay where we are. He's probably walking around right now, trying to find you. I bet if we stay put and keep our eyes open, we'll eventually spot him."

The girl looked a little dubious, but she gave a jerky nod.

A rowdy crowd of teenagers pushed past on the sidewalk then. As if worried she might get separated from an adult again, Caroline reached out to slide one sticky hand into Maddie's palm. Maternal feelings bubbled to the surface, poignant and bittersweet. There was something simple and satisfying about holding a child's hand, something both terrifying and humbling about knowing they depended on you, trusted you to do what was right and to keep them safe.

I don't deserve that trust, she thought, even as she

tightened her grip, forced a reassuring smile to her lips.

When the teens had passed, Caroline asked, "Why does your hand and arm look like this?"

Cam stumbled to a halt just yards away. His relief at finding his daughter in the safe care of Maddie Daniels turned to acute embarrassment over Caroline's appalling lack of manners. He was close enough to hear the question his daughter asked, but before he could chastise Caroline for being rude and make her apologize, Maddie answered—simply, honestly—and he found himself hanging on her every word.

"I was in a car accident a little over a year ago. It was a pretty bad accident, but the doctors at the hospital took good care of me."

"This musta hurt" came Caroline's solemn reply as she traced a finger over the scar. "Did you cry?"

"Yeah. I cried a lot." Maddie's voice was soft, sad, and to Cam's mortification, he found himself straining to hear it over the noise of the crowd.

"Is the accident why you walk kinda funny, too?"

Cam took a step forward, nearly into Maddie's line of vision. He wanted to spare her from answering any more uncomfortable questions, but curious himself, he eavesdropped some more when she began speaking.

"Yeah, I hurt my leg, too. The doctors had to fix it with metal pins in my knee and hip so that I could walk again."

"Metal pins? Do they get rusty? Is that why you walk so slow? I saw *The Wizard of Oz* once and this metal guy had to keep an oilcan with him because his knees and arms got rusty when it rained. Maybe you should carry one of those in your purse,'' she offered, all sincerity.

Relief flooded through Cam when he heard Maddie chuckle at his daughter's well-meaning solution, and he decided it was time to head off any further inquisition, no matter how enlightening he found it.

"There you are. You had me worried, sprite."

"Daddy!" she hollered as he scooped her up and planted a noisy kiss on her cheek. "You found us. Maddie said you would if we stayed put."

She beamed at her new friend.

"Hello, Maddie."

"Cameron." Stiff formality replaced the ease and animation with which she'd spoken to his daughter. He couldn't help but be disappointed with the change.

"Thanks for keeping an eye on the brat here." He tweaked his daughter's nose, delighting a giggle out of her. "I think I lost ten years off my life when I turned around and realized she had taken off."

"Really? The way I hear it, you were the one who wandered away," she admonished in sham seriousness. "You had Caroline quite worried."

Her teasing tone and the lightheartedness of her chiding surprised him. He hadn't known the woman possessed a sense of humor. Then again, he figured there was a lot about Maddie Daniels he didn't know.

"We're going to spend the day at the festival, Daddy promised." Then, in a single breath, Caroline announced, "He said I could eat all the cotton candy I wanted and go on rides and he's going to win me a big stuffed animal for my bedroom at home, something in pink because my room is pink.''

"That sounds like fun.''

The child grinned engagingly. "You wanna come with us?''

"Thank you, but I'm afraid I can't,'' Maddie declined with a polite shake of her head.

"Why not?'' Cam and Caroline asked in unison.

"Oh, well, I—I have work to do.''

Cam wasn't sure why, but he thought she was lying. "What work would that be? Finding me a date?''

"Yes, exactly.'' She seemed to sag with relief as she latched on to the excuse he provided.

He could have left it at that, probably should have, but for some reason he felt like pushing her. He wanted to see if she would retreat or engage in a verbal battle that might shed more light on the woman beneath all those stiff manners. Maddie puzzled him, that's all it was. That's why he'd thought about her so often over the past couple of days.

"Well, if you really want to get to know me better, discover all of those—what was the phrase you used that day in your office? 'Telling little quirks and habits' of mine—then you should spend the day with us. You're sure to get a better idea of my likes and dislikes that way than by asking a bunch of irrelevant questions.''

The gauntlet was down. He waited for her reply.

She arched an eyebrow, the one with the mole. She did that often, he noticed, when she was perplexed or irritated. It didn't say much about him, Cam was sure, but for some reason he liked knowing he could inspire both emotions in her.

"I might find out things you'd rather I didn't know," Maddie said.

He spread his arms wide. "Hey, my life's an open book. I've got nothing to hide."

"Everyone has something to hide, something they regret."

She smiled as she said it, but her tone seemed almost introspective. Before he could wonder about it, though, she added, "You're not a closet corn dog aficionado, are you?"

"Mmm, meat on a stick." He smacked his lips. "And named after a vegetable. That's two of the major food groups right there. I'm very health conscious. See, there's one of those little nuggets of information I promised. So, what do you say? I'll even pitch in for lunch. You don't look like you'll put much of a dent in my wallet."

He let his gaze meander over her slender frame, and felt an unmistakable current of interest charge through him. It shocked him just enough to have him almost hoping she would decline his invitation.

"We can ride the Tilt-A-Whirl," Caroline chirped enthusiastically, unaware of her father's sudden discomfort.

Maddie looked slightly green at the thought, but she smiled, anyway. "Not right after eating those corn dogs, I hope."

"Is that a yes?" Cam asked, still uncertain how he felt, but then her face brightened with a grin. It transformed her fragile beauty into something more substantial, and he realized it was the first time he'd seen her really smile. It reached her eyes, infusing a definite amount of warmth into their enigmatic blue depths, and it did something funny to his stomach.

"I'd be a fool to turn down the offer of meat on a stick, especially when you're going to buy."

The parade had ended, but the rest of the festival was in full swing. They walked to the midway where the rides teemed with screaming thrill-seekers who were both young and young-at-heart. Those feeling lucky tried their hands at games of skill and chance, trying to toss rings around milk jugs or land quarters on glass plates. The different aromas of cotton candy, popcorn, roasted peanuts and hot dogs mingled, and carnival workers leaned out of their concession booths to aggressively hawk their wares.

Maddie marveled at it all, taking it in, glad to be in the middle of it as long as Cam was nearby, solid and strong. Her hip and leg ached a bit. The walk from the parade route to the midway was much farther than she had expected to go.

But then, as they walked along, Cam took her hand and tucked it through his arm.

"Let me know when you get tired" was all he said, his tone matter-of-fact.

She felt something shift inside, found herself reevaluating him. He didn't give her any reason to feel awkward or embarrassed about her physical limitations. In fact, he appeared much more at ease with her disability than she sometimes was herself.

"It's not as hard to walk when I have something

to hold on to. I have a cane, I'm just too vain to use it," she said, surprising herself with the admission.

"With or without the cane, you're a beautiful woman, Maddie."

Judging by the way his cheeks turned a ruddy red, it seemed it was his turn to be surprised. Whether or not he had intended to offer the compliment, it warmed her. He couldn't see her leg or her hip and the ugly scarring there, or he certainly wouldn't have said it, but still, she'd take the kind words on any terms. It had been a long time since she'd heard such flattery from an attractive man. And Cameron Foley certainly was attractive.

"Thank you."

He shrugged, "Just stating fact."

Caroline piped up then, saving Maddie the bother of untying her tongue.

"Hey, there's Aunt Eve!"

She skipped ahead, but Cameron didn't so much as hasten his stride. His steps remained slow, measured and sure as he guided Maddie through the crowd to a strikingly handsome couple that stood with Caroline and two adorable boys.

"Maddie Daniels, this is Eve and Richard Jakes. Eve is my sister-in-law."

"It's nice to meet you."

Angela's sister, Maddie decided, assessing the woman's seemingly flawless features for clues about Cameron's late wife. If Angela had been half as attractive as her sibling, she'd been utterly stunning. Eve's dark hair was styled in a sleek bob that followed the delicate curve of her jaw. Her eyes were brown, a shade lighter than her hair, and tipped up at the corners. With her full lips and full figure, she reminded Maddie of Sophia Loren despite the casual khaki shorts and white tank top she wore.

Caroline tugged at Maddie's hand, eager to finish the introductions.

"These are my cousins, Trevor and Tucker. They're both eight 'cause they're twins. Sometimes Daddy has a hard time telling them apart, but not me," she confided importantly.

The twins had sandy-blond hair, the same shade as their father's, and the sun had dusted a trail of freckles over their noses. They smiled politely at Maddie, but she thought she caught a bit of the devil dancing in the brown eyes that dominated their round faces.

"We're going on the Sea Dragon. You've got to be this tall," Trevor said, holding a hand to his forehead. "Sorry, Caroline, you're too small."

"Yeah, you're just a baby," Tucker chimed in, giving one of her pigtails a yank.

"No one is going on the Sea Dragon," Eve said mildly, clearly a pro at stopping arguments before they could start. She turned to Cameron. "So, how long have you two known each other?"

Cameron seemed to take the question at face value, but Maddie had been in business long enough to hear all of the nuances to a query like that. The woman was curious about more than the length of their acquaintance.

"Not long," he said with a shrug.

"Ah. I'm surprised you didn't mention you were meeting someone here today."

"I didn't meet Maddie here…exactly. We ran into each other at the parade when I went in search of Caroline. Maddie was kind enough to keep an eye on the sprite until I could find her. I'm paying her back with a corn dog." He grinned at Maddie over the inside joke, unaware of the look that passed between Eve and Richard.

Maddie wasn't unaware. She knew speculation when she saw it.

"Paying her back is right," Richard said with a laugh.

"Honestly, Cam, you've been out of circulation way too long if you think greasy carnival fare can be considered an acceptable date," Eve added.

"We're not dating," Cam sputtered, at the same time Maddie hastily corrected her. "Oh, this isn't a date."

Maddie quickly withdrew her hand from the crook of Cam's arm.

"Actually, I'm working on finding Cameron a date. It's what I do for a living. I, um, find people dates." Maddie hoped she sounded professional, but she was sure she was blushing. For some reason she felt like a teenager caught necking on the family sofa.

Cameron offered desperately, "Yeah. She's my matchmaker."

"A matchmaker?" Eve squeaked. She looked appalled, and Maddie swore Cameron winced. His sister-in-law's voice rose an octave when she continued. "Oh, my God! I know I've been rather outspoken on the issue of you dating again. And I still think it's time for you to start socializing. But I didn't mean to pressure you into joining an…an escort service.''

''Dating service,'' Maddie said stiffly, well aware of the ugly assumptions some people made about her line of work.

Richard lightened the moment considerably with his unexpected shout of laughter.

''Dear,'' he said, when he finally caught his breath. ''If I'm not mistaken, this proper-looking and Southern-sounding lady thinks you've accused her of being Cam's pimp.''

''What's a pimp?'' the boys chimed in unison.

''Yeah, what's a pimp?'' Caroline wanted to know.

''Thanks,'' Cam muttered, rubbing a hand over his forehead. ''Like I'm ready to explain *that* one to her. We're still a few years away from the birds and bees.''

Richard settled the matter quickly by pulling a crisp twenty-dollar bill out of his wallet and handing it to one of the twins.

''The three of you go buy some more cotton candy.'' As they streaked away with an earsplitting whoop of joy, he hollered after them, ''And I expect change!''

''Sorry about that,'' Eve said when the children were gone. ''I didn't mean it like it sounded. I'm sure you run a perfectly legal and respectable business. It's just that I have someone…'' She stopped, smiled sheepishly.

''You have someone you want Cameron to meet,'' Maddie finished for her.

''What?'' Cam took Eve's hand and squeezed it.

"Honey, I appreciate the thought, really I do. Especially since I know how close you were to Angie. But I've told you a dozen times, I'm not interested in dating anyone."

"Okay…" Richard frowned. "You've lost me."

"Yes. Why join a dating service if you're not interested in dating?" Eve asked.

"I didn't join Maddie's service."

That clarified nothing for his baffled in-laws. So Maddie said, "We have a deal—a wager, really. Cameron doesn't believe I can introduce him to a woman he'll be interested in seeing a second time. I have until Valentine's Day to prove him wrong."

"Or what?" Richard asked.

"The terms of our wager aren't really important," Maddie evaded.

"She's right," Cam agreed. "What's important is that I'm going to win."

Maddie turned to Eve. "Has he always been this arrogant?"

"Oh, he's mellowed some over the years."

"That's scary. I can't imagine what's worse than being insufferable."

"Hey, no need to talk about me as if I'm not here," Cam inserted. "Keep it up and I may take back my offer to pay for your lunch."

"Ooh, that should bring her right into line," Eve said dryly. "There's little a woman won't do for a corn dog."

"Really?" One of his brows winged up and his expression turned comically wolfish. "That so? I guess things have changed since I last dated."

"Things have changed, all right," Richard agreed. "You wouldn't believe how aggressive some single women can be." The comment earned him a how-do-you-know glare from his wife, and he amended, "I mean, that's what I hear, anyway."

"I'm sure Maddie will take good care of me." He smiled at her when he said it, and squeezed her hand before tucking it back into the crook of his arm. It was a chivalrous gesture, nothing more, but her heart took a funny leap at the contact.

The children came rushing back, saving her from saying something foolish. Their faces and hands were pink and sticky from what was left of their airy confections.

"Daddy, Trevor and Tucker said they're going to go trout fishing. Can I go, too?"

"Trout fishing?"

"They have a couple of ponds set up over by the Open Space for the kids," Eve explained. "You know she's welcome to come along with us."

Turning back to his daughter, he asked, "What are you going to do if you catch a fish?"

Tucker piped up for her, taking great delight in answering. "Well, you can keep it, gut it and cook it, or donate it to the zoo where it will be used for bear food."

"I'm going to free it," Caroline announced proudly. "I'm going to dump it right into the bay so that it can swim away and find a family. So, if you let me go with them, Daddy, you'll be saving a fish's life."

"Oh, she is good," Maddie whispered, camouflaging her chuckle with a cough.

"Takes after her mother," Cameron replied. He gave his daughter some money and a kiss for luck.

As Eve and Richard walked to the trout pond, Richard asked his wife, "So, what do you think they wagered? Stakes must be pretty high if neither one of them is willing to talk about it."

"They're high, all right," Eve replied. Her tone was troubled when she added, "Judging from the way she looked at Cam, I think Maddie Daniels wagered her heart."

"Really? Do you think Cam knows?"

"No. In fact, I don't think either one of them has figured it out yet."

Chapter Four

Despite being surrounded by the milling crowd, Maddie felt conspicuously alone with Cameron once the others had gone. Perhaps some of the lingering awkwardness she felt was because of Eve's initial assumption that Maddie was Cameron's date. Sure, she enjoyed the way her hand was tucked into the crook of his muscular arm. It made her feel cared for, secure, protected, and she hadn't felt that way in a very long time. But she knew better than to romanticize the old-fashioned gesture or read too much into it. Cam was just being polite. Even as she reached that conclusion, he untucked her hand and slid his arm around her waist.

Startled, she glanced up in question.

"What are you doing?"

"Ground's pretty uneven here." He nodded toward a stretch of buckled asphalt in front of them. "I just wanted to have a tight hold on you."

You already seem to, came the stray thought. *Absurd,* she told herself, pushing it away. *Absolutely absurd.*

"You might want to hold on to me, too." His lips twitched as he added, "We wouldn't want a repeat of what happened in my orchard."

That appalling thought had her winding an arm around Cam's taut midsection. Even as she told herself she was just being practical, her pulse picked up speed. Maddie was so intent on trying to appear nonchalant, she wasn't aware that her index finger had threaded through one of the loops at the waistband of his jeans until he said with an embarrassed chuckle, "I usually wear a belt, but Caroline had me up and out the door so early this morning, I'm lucky I got a chance to shave. She wanted to have a front-row seat at the parade."

"Kids love parades," she whispered hoarsely, discreetly withdrawing the errant finger.

"What about you?" He leaned down as he said it and his jaw brushed her temple.

"What's not to like?"

"Yeah." It was his voice that sounded hoarse now.

They had successfully navigated the potholed patch, so there was no need for the additional support. Maddie quickly disentangled herself from their quasi-embrace. Eager for something neutral to say as he once again took her hand and placed it on his arm, she asked, "How are your cherries coming? Have you picked any yet?"

"We don't actually pick them. We shake the trees with a machine."

"Shake them?"

"Yeah. The machine looks like a big upside down umbrella. It makes the work less tedious, and while it might sound sadistic," he said with a grin, "it doesn't hurt the trees or bruise the fruit."

"Oh." Another uncomfortable silence ensued before Maddie asked, "Are some of your cherries sold over there?"

She pointed to the area near the waterfront just across Highway 31 that was referred to as the Open Space. In addition to the booths set up by area restaurants to sell sandwiches and other more filling food than what was available on the midway, a huge tent was set up with vendors hawking all things cherry. There were cherry pies, cherry turnovers, cherry cookies, tarts and scones. Cherry butter, cherry jam, cherry salsa, even cherry mustard. There were dried cherries, chocolate-covered cherries and, of course, loose, washed sweet cherries ready to be popped into one's mouth. Plenty already had, if the number of pits dotting the grounds was any indication.

"No. The tarts don't make good eating fresh, but they're great for pies and jams and such. The sweets are what are sold over there, but most of my harvest will be sent to a canning company." He slanted her a grin that was dangerously charming. "Think of me next time you eat a sundae with a maraschino cherry on top."

Her mouth went dry, but she managed to keep her tone light when she replied, "Ah, the maraschino cherry. What would a sundae be without one? But don't you sell any of your crop fresh?"

He smiled again, absently this time, at what she was sure was a fond memory.

"When Angie was alive, we sold pints and quarts from a stand out by the road. She got a kick out of talking to people. I swear that she ate and gave away more cherries than she ever sold."

Although he didn't seem overly troubled by the recollection, Maddie searched for something else to talk about. She mentally kicked herself when she blurted out, "I haven't found you a match yet."

Cameron didn't seem bothered by the statement. In fact, he seemed rather pleased.

"I didn't figure you had. But don't worry. There's no rush."

"Easy for you to say," she grumbled.

"Yes, it is."

He flashed another irresistible grin that had her forgetting how irritating his arrogance could be. Smiling or scowling, he really was quite handsome. He had the kind of face that warranted a second glance, and many of the women at the festival were doing just that. Maddie sized them up with a critical eye—that was her business, after all—and found them all falling short in one way or another. Finding Cameron Foley a match was going to prove difficult, especially given his rather narrow list of preferences.

"What are you thinking about?" he asked.

She shrugged. "Nothing important. So, where's my corn dog? That's one bargain I won't let you worm your way out of."

"Oh, I'll pay up, but I'm thinking we ought to take

in the sights first.'' He stopped walking and pointed up. ''From there.''

Maddie craned her neck and felt her stomach drop to her toes. The double Ferris wheel seemed to shoot up a couple dozen stories into the cloudless summer sky, and the seats swayed with almost nauseating ease.

''I—I don't know. I'm not much on heights.''

He cocked his head to one side. ''I'd have never taken you for a chicken, Maddie.''

She knew a challenge when she heard one and generally didn't care to back down, but squinting up at the ride gave her pause. She would put self-preservation before pride any day.

''The merry-go-round is really more my speed.''

He shook his head and snorted in feigned disgust. ''Where's your sense of adventure, Daniels? I'm willing to let you set me up with God only knows who. The least you can do is go on a ride with me. Come on. Caroline would go if she were here and she's only six.''

''That's low.''

''What can I say? I'm ruthless.'' He sent her a wink. ''Better write that down in my file, too.''

He didn't give her a chance to protest further. He grabbed her hand and gently but firmly pulled her along behind him as he bought the tickets and then got in line.

''I don't think this is a good idea, Cameron,'' she objected weakly for the tenth time as a disreputable-looking carnival worker snugged a metal bar over their laps. The thin stick of metal didn't look secure.

Indeed, the entire car looked rickety and unsafe when viewed through the eyes of fear.

"I—I can't do this."

She tugged at the bar, but it didn't budge. It reminded her a bit too much of the way the steering wheel had pinned her inside her car during those brief moments of terror before she'd lost consciousness.

"Maddie, live a little," Cameron teased, unaware of her building panic. "The view from the top will be worth a little vertigo, I promise. I think Grand Traverse Bay is one of the prettiest places on the planet. All those varying shades of blue."

"Shades of blue," she repeated inanely, swallowing against the nausea that crept up the back of her throat.

"Yeah, everything from aqua to midnight, depending on the depth of the water. I don't think the Caribbean has anything on Lake Michigan, except warmer water. But then, we don't have sharks, either," he added with a chuckle.

She tried to laugh, too, but the car lurched and climbed several feet. Maddie made a desperate grab for the bar.

"Cameron!"

"Don't worry. This isn't the Tilt-A-Whirl or a roller coaster. It will be a slow ride, I promise."

The cadence of his voice was even and sincere. One of his arms dangled over the side of their car and he sat with his legs crossed at the ankles, the picture of relaxation. He obviously felt the ride was safe. Maddie tried to will the tension in her muscles to slacken.

"I like things that go slow," she said, gritting her teeth only slightly.

He turned and smiled at her. "I like things that go slow, too. Nice and slow."

His gaze connected with hers, held for one intense moment. Maddie wasn't sure if it was the way he looked at her or the swaying motion of the ride that caused her stomach to flutter. The Ferris wheel jerked again, turning higher so that more passengers could be loaded into the cars below. The raucous sounds of the carnival sifted into the background.

Cameron Foley had the most amazing eyes, coffee brown with random flecks of gold dotting the outer edges. From the corners, deep lines fanned out to his temples. They were from squinting into the sun, as he was doing now. And from smiling. He was doing that now, too, and it drew her gaze to his mouth. *I bet he's a fabulous kisser.* The thought came from nowhere. She wondered if maybe she'd spoken it aloud when he began to lean toward her. For one thrilling, terrifying moment, she thought their mouths would meet.

She felt his breath, warm and feather-light, caress her cheek when he asked, "Are you scared?"

Maddie let out the breath she hadn't been aware of holding. "Why should I be scared?"

His serious expression dissolved into a wicked grin. "Because here we go."

The car plunged over the edge, taking Maddie's stomach with it. She stared out at vast nothingness for one seemingly eternal moment before the crowded midway came into view. She gripped the safety bar, her knuckles turning white. It's just a ride, she told herself, but she felt dizzy and out of control as first the ground and then the blue sky glided past her. She'd felt this way before, when her car had skidded and rolled on the rain-slicked two-lane road after colliding with a log-hauling semi. She closed her eyes and clenched her teeth as painful memories flooded back.

Other riders were screaming around them, but Maddie heard only her own scream from that night fifteen months earlier. It seemed to echo in her head. It was one of the few things she remembered clearly about the accident. That and the pain. She clenched her eyes shut.

"Come on, Maddie, open your eyes. You're missing the best part. The view is great."

Beside her, Cam poked his elbow into her ribs, trying to get a rise out of her. He'd have never taken her for such a baby. But then he caught a glimpse of her face. It was pasty white, misted with a fine sweat.

"Maddie?"

Cam didn't think, he acted. Going on instinct, he put his arm around her, pulled her trembling body tight against his. Resting his chin atop her head, he rubbed his hand down her shuddering back, comforting her as he might Caroline, even as his body's reaction told him he held a woman, not a child.

"It's okay. It's okay. We're slowing down. It's almost over."

"It will never be over," she said with such sad certainty that he knew she was talking about more than a carnival ride. But he didn't ask what. He couldn't. He'd pushed her too far already. Why was it, he wondered, that this one woman had the ability to bring out the absolute worst in him?

"Your girlfriend looks a little green," the worker commented with a snide little chuckle when it came time for them to exit the ride. Cam felt like giving the little silver hoop that protruded from the guy's left eyebrow a quick, hard yank. He settled for sending him a black look and helped Maddie out of the seat.

With his arm around her waist, he escorted her down the ramp to firmer ground, and then away from the crowds. He eased her onto the small metal steps on the back of a concession trailer. When she was seated, she didn't look at him. Instead, she dropped her head into her hands and seemed to struggle to catch her breath.

"You must think I'm an idiot," she said weakly a moment later.

Cam crouched down in front of her, relieved to see the faintest hint of color rising on those high cheekbones when she finally raised her head.

"Not at all. I'm the idiot. You said you didn't want to go on the ride, but I all but forced you onto it. I'm sorry, Maddie."

It seemed natural, necessary even, to touch her. He brushed back her hair so that he could see that fascinating little mole. His palm lingered against smooth skin that felt clammy and was still far too pale for his liking.

"Want me to take you home now?"

She shook her head, seemed to collect herself. "No. I'm fine. I just need a minute."

"Sure. Take all the time you need." He dropped down beside her on the small step, their bodies touching, shoulder to shoulder and thigh to thigh. She was such a small thing, really. Fragile—the word came to him again. He told himself that was why he put his arm around her and gave her a reassuring squeeze.

"I'm sorry, Maddie," he said again.

He could feel the slight shudders still working their way through her, but her tone was even and valiantly upbeat when she replied, "Buy me lunch and we'll call it even. Then, if you're still feeling guilty, you can walk me back to my office. There's some paperwork I really do need to finish up today."

Cam agreed. What else could he do? Yet, it bothered him immensely to realize Maddie would be spending the rest of a beautiful Saturday cooped up in her office.

When they reached the Open Space, the crowd was thicker but seemed less boisterous. A brightly dressed clown passed, playing a kazoo, and a group of delighted children tagged after him as if he were a pied piper. Their parents, toting video cameras and armloads of festival contraband, brought up the rear.

"How about chicken gyros?" Cam asked at the same time Maddie said, "Oh, the U&I Lounge has a booth again this year."

"A meeting of the minds," he replied with a grin. "I've been known to drive in to Traverse just to have one of their gyros."

"You have excellent taste, then. I'll be sure to note

that in your file. They do make the best sandwiches around. The secret is the dill," she confided.

She sounded a bit like a connoisseur. Did she eat out often, Cam wondered? She seemed so wedded to her job that he wouldn't be surprised to find that she regularly dined on take-out. He'd eaten his share of fast-food burgers and home-delivered pizzas after Angie's death. All he could think was, how lonely.

The tables were filled, so Cam suggested they walk over by the band shell where other people had stretched out on the grass to enjoy food and music. A country-western group was warming up for an afternoon concert. The strum of guitar strings and squawk of a fiddle rose above the crowd noise, luring others away from the food court. He consulted his watch—twelve-fifteen—then looked around to find the bright red Chevy Tahoe that would be raffled later in the week. Eve and the gang had promised to meet him there at one.

"How about here?" Since his hands were occupied with the tray, he motioned with his chin to a flat, cherry-pit free patch of earth where the grass had been trampled to a brownish-green carpet.

"This will be fine."

Cam knelt down, setting the tray of food and drinks between them.

He glanced up at Maddie. "Need any help?"

She shook her head. "Down is fine. It's the up part I have trouble with." The smile she sent him was only slightly embarrassed as she gingerly lowered herself to the ground.

"I overheard what you told Caroline. About the accident, I mean. It must have been pretty bad, huh?"

"Pretty bad," she agreed, becoming absorbed in unwrapping her sandwich. She took a bite of the gyro. After chewing and swallowing, she said, "You know, at the pub, they'll add feta cheese if you ask."

He decided to let her get away with changing the subject. For now. Cam couldn't say why, but he wanted to know more. He needed to sort out all of the puzzling pieces that added up to one interesting Maddie Daniels. He decided if he could figure out what it was that intrigued him, he would stop thinking about her so often.

They ate their sandwiches and sipped their colas while the band played its version of a Garth Brooks tune. Cam leaned back on his elbows, stretched out his legs on the grass and crossed his ankles. Maddie couldn't strike a similar pose, so she hooked her arm around one bent knee, leaving the other leg straight. As covertly as possible, she studied Cameron.

Maddie had thought she had him pegged after their first couple of meetings, but he continued to surprise her. He was a man capable of interesting conversations as well as companionable silences. Depending on his mood, he could be intense or lighthearted, arrogant or humble. That reckless, wicked grin, which surely had caused many a woman to sigh in feminine appreciation, could dissolve without warning into compassionate understanding. He was all man—solid muscle packaged in faded denim—but, judging from Caroline's crooked pigtails, he wasn't above using those big, callused hands to style a little girl's hair.

He drank domestic beer but preferred French wine. He could be as abrasive as sandpaper, as cold as the bay in February, or unbearably sweet. He'd been all three with Maddie during their short acquaintance, and she wasn't at all sure which she found most disturbing.

"Let me know if you're uncomfortable in that position. We can walk around some if you start feeling stiff."

"I'm fine," she replied, even as her heart knocked clumsily. And she had her answer. Abrasive she could deal with. Cold she could endure. His sweetness, however, made her nervous. It made her yearn for things she could not have, things she did not deserve.

"Are you going to finish that?"

Startled, she met his gaze. He motioned to the half-eaten sandwich she held in one hand.

"I guess I'm not that hungry after all. Would you like it?"

He grinned in response, and took the gyro without so much as token resistance. No one would call Cameron Foley bashful when it came to food. He finished the sandwich in a few quick bites, licking his fingers afterward. She found herself staring at his mouth again, fascinated.

He must have noticed the direction of her gaze, because he said, "Did I leave any evidence?"

Maddie didn't know what possessed her, but she raised her hand, resting the palm lightly against his cheek, and with the pad of her thumb pretended to brush away nonexistent crumbs. He leaned forward slightly and so did she, bringing their faces into surprisingly close proximity. Vaguely, Maddie heard the shriek of a fiddle and the thump of boot heels on the stage as the band kicked off another up-tempo tune. But neither she nor Cameron moved. Her hand still rested on his cheek, and his eyes were clouded with some indecipherable emotion. They seemed frozen in time, the only two people on the planet, until he finally closed the gap and gently settled his mouth over hers. He tasted like dill and…heaven.

Maddie had been kissed before. She'd been married, after all, and before that she'd dated some. But this was like being struck by lightning—quite simply, nothing else compared. The kiss was soft, almost tentative. His mouth lingered over hers, hesitated a brief, blissful moment before he pulled away.

What am I doing? Cam wondered. Some primitive and nearly forgotten urge charged through him. It was about as welcome as a rabid dog, but he was no teenager at the mercy of unruly hormones. He was an adult, a man who could deal with an unwanted surge of sexual attraction. With a shaky hand, he picked up his soft drink, sipped and told himself this attraction did not really exist. And if it did exist, it really didn't matter. It just meant that three years was an awfully long time for a man to go without female companionship.

"Sun's hot," he said inanely, giving his paper cup a shake that had the ice cubes tinkling.

Maddie willed her breathing to slow from hyperventilation range. More than the sun was hot, she thought, welcoming the breeze that blew in from the bay.

Then she felt slapped by a blast of Arctic air when a familiar voice called from behind her, "I didn't know you went for public displays of affection, Madison."

She turned her head slowly, but even knowing the identity of the speaker, she wasn't prepared to see him. Her ex-husband looked as tanned and fit and handsome as ever. He wore a designer polo shirt and a pair of white tennis shorts. A sweater was casually looped over his shoulders. With his sun-bleached blond hair and aristocratic good looks, he belonged on the cover of a yachting magazine.

She schooled her expression into one of polite indifference. "Hello, Ted."

"I'd heard you lived in the area. Of course, you always did like Traverse City better than Grosse Pointe, even in the dead of winter."

She nodded stiffly, vaguely defensive even though he only stated fact, and struggled to stand. Cameron was beside her in an instant, solicitously helping her to her feet.

"I took a place in town," she replied.

A place so small it could fit into the foyer of the massive home she and Ted had once shared in one of Detroit's toniest suburbs. Even his so-called summerhouse, which boasted a stunning view of the bay, had walk-in closets larger than her dinky kitchenette.

"Ah, well, Lauren and I made the trip up this weekend for the festival."

He motioned to his right, and for the first time Maddie noticed the woman standing beside him. She'd heard, of course, that Ted had remarried, mere weeks, as it happened, after their speedy divorce became final nine months earlier. The timing sometimes made her wonder about his fidelity, but she told herself she was happy for him, happy that he'd moved on with his life.

Enough of Ted's friends had places in the area that she ran into them on occasion. Despite their sympathetic words, they seemed to take great delight in telling Maddie all about her ex-husband's new life. This, however, was the first time she'd seen him since their date in court, and it became immediately apparent that Ted's chatty friends had neglected to mention one heart-stopping detail of Ted's bride. The woman was everything Maddie would never be: perky, petite. Pregnant. Maddie's heart squeezed most painfully when her gaze dropped to Lauren's slightly rounded abdomen and the protective hand the woman rested there.

From some faraway place she heard Ted making the perfunctory introductions, and she was aware of the quizzical gaze Cameron shot her as he shook the hand Ted extended.

"I hear you opened a dating service," Ted said. There was a sneering tone to his voice, but his face remained impassive.

She offered a smile that she hoped didn't look as brittle as it felt.

"Yes. True Love, Incorporated. I opened it just before the finalization of our..." Her gaze slid briefly to Cameron before she finished with, "About a year ago. I believe I told you about it then."

Ted's smile was patronizing. "Perhaps that's where I heard it. I guess you have to make a living."

That went without saying since she'd walked away from their marriage with little more than the clothes in her closet, a totaled car and twenty-five grand from their joint checking account. He'd gotten both houses, the Mercedes, their impressive stock portfolio and other assorted investments. Ted hadn't had to hire an attorney to secure these things. Maddie had given them up eagerly, gladly. They were just material possessions, and even when added together, they didn't come close to repaying Ted for what had been lost, for what Maddie had cost him.

"I have an office downtown. It's doing very well, I think. The area is growing by leaps and bounds. At this point I don't have much competition."

"You've turned into quite the entrepreneur, although I'll admit to being surprised. I wouldn't think you would consider this kind of service to be your…forte."

Cam didn't know quite what was going on or who this Ted character was, but he knew he didn't like the man. And he knew an insult when he heard one, even if it was offered through straight white teeth and in perfectly enunciated syllables.

He waited for Maddie to exhibit some of the backbone she'd shown with him when he'd said something to tick her off, but to his amazement, she allowed this annoyingly smug man to get away with the slight about her business.

"It suits me," she answered. "I'm surprised to see

you here. I didn't think you liked to do touristy things when you stay at the summer house.''

"Well, Lauren's never been to the Cherry Festival. I tried to tell her she wasn't missing much, but she wanted to see for herself.'' He wrapped an arm around his young bride, pulling her close. "In her condition, I prefer to indulge her.''

"I'm very happy for you.'' Cam watched Maddie swallow, then moisten her lips before continuing. "I know how much you want children.''

Ted smiled, his eyes as flat and cold as a shark's. "Yes, I believe you do.''

Something seemed almost threatening about the way he said it. Cam waited until the pair was out of earshot to ask, "Who was that jerk?''

He didn't bother to wonder whether he had a right to demand such information, or to insult someone she obviously knew quite well. Nor could he say why he suddenly felt so protective. But Maddie didn't seem perturbed by his gruff tone. Her gaze followed the couple as they made there way through the crowd to the souvenir tent. She seemed preoccupied when she replied, "He's my ex-husband.''

"Ex-husband?'' Cam sputtered, feeling as if he'd just taken a good, solid jab to his solar plexus.

She'd been married? And to that…that stuffed shirt? Wealthy stuffed shirt, he amended. Cam didn't have much use for designer clothes, but that didn't mean he didn't recognize them. What Ted paid for his natty man-of-leisure duds would have set Cam back a couple of truck payments.

Maddie seemed to snap out of her trance. Embarrassment colored her cheeks.

"Some matchmaker I am, huh?" she said sheepishly. "I failed at marriage. I know how much stock you put into sticking it out even through the worst of times. I wasn't able to do that."

I, Cam noticed. Not we. She accepted the blame for the divorce, but he couldn't believe she deserved all of it, especially since her ex had obviously landed quickly on his feet if his young, pregnant bride was any indication.

Cam watched Maddie nibble her lower lip—a lip he now knew from personal experience was as soft as it looked.

Something told him Maddie had tried to honor her marriage vows. And for just the slightest moment he found himself relieved, indeed, glad, she hadn't been successful. It was because the man was such a jerk, he told himself.

"How long...?" He wasn't sure what he wanted to know, so he just let the question hang there.

"How long was I married? Five years. How long have I been divorced? Officially, less than one. Ted left right after..." She blinked rapidly, looked away.

"After your accident," he finished for her.

She nodded, looking so miserable he didn't have the heart to press her further, even though he was curious. What kind of man left a woman immediately after she'd suffered serious injuries? And what kind of woman allowed him to do so without being bitter afterward? From what he could tell, Maddie Daniels wasn't bitter or angry toward her ex-husband. She just looked sad, incredibly sad.

And, oddly enough, guilty.

A week later, Cam was putting Caroline to bed when the telephone rang. He planted a hasty kiss on his daughter's forehead and dashed to find the cordless. On the fourth ring, he located it, hidden beneath a pile of newspapers next to his favorite recliner.

"Hello?" he rasped, winded from his frantic search.

"Cameron, I hope I'm not calling at a bad time. It's Maddie Daniels."

She gave her full name as if he could have forgotten her in the span of a week. The number of times during the past seven days that Cam had thought about that one brief, ill-advised kiss proved this was not a woman who would be forgotten easily.

"What's up?"

"Well, I know it's after hours, but this is actually an official call."

"Official?" For the briefest moment, he felt disappointed.

"Yes. I found you a date, Cameron."

She always did that, he thought, said his full name in that proper-sounding way of hers. It made him smile.

"A date, huh? What's her name?"

"Francine Lyons. She's twenty-four, never married. Blond, five-eight, one hundred and thirty-five pounds. Oh, and she has small feet and trim ankles," she added with what sounded like a chuckle.

"You've been busy."

"Of course, I'll understand if you don't trust my judgment. I am…" She cleared her throat. "I am divorced. Are you sure you still trust me to find you a date?"

Here was his out, but he couldn't take it. "We had a deal, Maddie. You trying to welsh already? I never figured you for a quitter."

He swore he heard her sigh in relief.

"Eight o'clock Friday. You're meeting her at that new karaoke bar near the college—Stargazers. Know the one?"

"I know the one," he replied. He'd driven past it a few times, although he'd never been inside.

"Good. Casual attire. Oh, what's your favorite color?"

"Red."

"Cherry red?" Her tone held humor and he wondered if one of those rare smiles might be tugging at her lips.

"That would be the shade."

"Good. Your date will be wearing it."

Chapter Five

Cam felt like a fool, or at the very least like a teen-ager in the throes of first-date angst. He'd changed his clothes three times, finally settling on a pair of new blue jeans and a white button-down shirt that Mrs. Haversham had dutifully ironed before leaving for the day. He'd traded in his steel-toed work boots for a pair of loafers that he managed to dig out of the back of his closet. After he wiped off the dust and applied a coat of polish, they looked almost new. And he'd even shaved a second time for the day before slapping on some spicy-smelling cologne that he hadn't worn in years.

But he didn't want to go on the date. He'd racked his brain for a reason good enough to call it off and stay home, but unfortunately he couldn't come up with one. And even if he had, he probably would have gone anyway. He'd made a promise to Maddie, and he was a man of his word—even if it didn't suit him to be at the moment.

In the midst of his crisis, Eve arrived to pick up Caroline, who would be staying overnight at her house. His sister-in-law whistled through her teeth when he walked into the living room.

"You look handsome," she said, then stepped closer to sniff. "And you smell good, too."

He shoved an impatient hand through his hair, feeling foolish for having had it cut just that afternoon.

"Do you think this is okay for a karaoke bar?"

"It's fine. Casual but classic." She smiled, wagged her eyebrows. "And, of course, you wear jeans so well, Cam."

He felt himself blush.

"You're not supposed to notice that, Eve. My God, we're family."

"By marriage," she reminded him. Then she cleared her throat. "Speaking of which, Cam, are you going to wear that?"

He followed the direction of her gaze to his left ring finger.

"I think it's time you considered taking it off," she said. "It doesn't mean you didn't love Angie. I know you did. More important, *she* knew it."

He said nothing, just eyed the thick gold band. Since the day he'd stormed into Maddie's office, he hadn't removed it, even when he'd been literally up to his elbows in cherries.

"It's been three years," Eve said. "Angie would want you to go on. She'd want you to be happy again."

"I am happy."

His sister-in-law just arched an eyebrow at that.

"I still love her."

The words came out a little belligerent. Eve smiled sympathetically and reached out to give his hand a squeeze.

"Of course you do. I still love her, too." Her smile turned melancholy. "But I found someone else to go with me on my annual all-day Christmas shopping adventure downstate."

"That's not the same."

"No, it's not," she agreed quietly. "The holes that her death left in our lives are very different. My point is, she would be miserable knowing we were miserable."

True enough. Angie had been bighearted and giving. He fiddled with the ring for a moment before slipping it off and stuffing it into the front pocket of his jeans. He wanted it close by just in case he changed his mind.

"I guess I'm as ready as I'll ever be. Thanks for watching the munchkin tonight."

"You're welcome. You know I love to have her at the house. After all, the boys do nothing but complain when I paint their toenails."

"I'll try to call her to say good-night when I get home."

He hollered for Caroline, then leaned over and kissed Eve on the cheek.

"I don't plan to be late."

Stargazers was packed with people, the majority of them fudgies, judging by the Traverse City-themed

T-shirts they wore. Cam bought a beer at the bar and managed to drink half of it before turning to survey the throng of gyrating patrons. He wasn't above enlisting the aid of a little false courage. He felt he needed it to face his first date with a woman other than Angela in too many years to count.

He thought about Maddie and the day they had spent at the Cherry Festival. That, of course, hadn't been a date. They had merely enjoyed each other's company. And, he admitted, they'd begun a rather interesting friendship, all things considered. Sure, there had been that one strange, stirring kiss, but it had been a mistake, an accident.

But this was a date, and a blind date to boot. His palms felt damp just thinking about it. He glanced around the room again and spied a red-clad blonde working her way through the crowd. She was a knockout, no denying that, with a long mane of honey-colored hair, lush full lips and exotically tilted green eyes. She had a heavy hand when it came to makeup, but when it came to clothing she obviously subscribed to the ''less is more'' theory. The skimpy excuse for a dress clung to her shapely form like a second skin, exposing far more of her than it managed to cover. He swallowed thickly while his gaze cruised over her curves. He doubted many lingerie models were built like that, and he couldn't help wondering what parts were real and what parts had been augmented.

He chugged the rest of his beer before she reached him at the bar.

"You must be Cameron." She used his full name, just as Maddie always did, but her voice wasn't slow, smoky or Southern-sounding. It was a husky purr that vibrated from her throat and made a man think of sex. Of course, everything about this woman made a man think of sex. She was a walking billboard for carnal knowledge, and he couldn't help but recall just how long it had been since he'd lost himself in a woman's soft curves.

"Maddie's snapshot didn't do you justice. You're a lot...stronger-looking in person." She reached out to trail one bloodred fingernail intimately up his forearm, and Cam's mind went alarmingly blank. So he said the first thing that popped into it.

"I'm a cherry farmer."

She smiled, obviously aware of her impact on men. Ripe lips bowed in unmistakable invitation.

"I know. And that's such a coincidence since cherries are my favorite fruit. I'm Francine Lyons." She leaned forward and he was sure it was her intention to rest that impressive bosom against his arm. "My friends call me Francie. I hope by the end of the evening we'll be much more than just friends."

This was moving too fast. Much too fast. They seemed to have skipped all of the first-date formalities he remembered. Instead they had gone straight to the "my place or yours?" part. He took a step back and briefly considered bolting for the exit. He must be out of his mind to be here. At the very least, he knew he was out of his league. Francine Lyons was an Indy car and he was used to slower, less flashy modes of transportation. For some reason, Maddie popped into his mind.

"Why don't we see if we can get a table?" he said at last.

"If that's what you really want." Again, the inviting smile curved her lips, and he had to bite his own to keep his mouth from gaping open. Why did this woman need a dating service? He'd bet she could snap her fingers and any one of the dozen drooling men standing near them would follow her out the door.

"Table," he repeated, adding a vigorous nod.

There was only one table left, and it was next to the swinging double doors that led to the kitchen. Francine sat as close to him as she could without actually plopping down on his lap, and then, unbelievably, he felt her fingers skim over his inner thigh. He jumped, camouflaging his nervous reaction by raising a hand to motion for the waitress.

"Could we see a couple of menus, please? And I'll take another beer when you get a chance." Was that his voice? It sounded at least a couple of octaves too high.

When the waitress left, Cam decided conversation was his best bet. "So, what made you join a dating service?"

"I have such a hard time meeting nice men." Francine pouted briefly before adding, "You're nice, aren't you, Cameron?"

"I'd like to think so."

"I'm glad," she purred. "Because you know what I'm really hungry for right now?"

"Can't imagine," he mumbled. *Where was that beer?*

"Dessert." And her wayward hand struck again.

My God! What kind of woman had Maddie set him up with? But, of course, Cam knew. Francine Lyons was just as he'd described his ideal woman: blond, beautiful, long legs, large chest and probably just out of college—assuming she'd even gone.

Cam suffered through an hour of vapid conversation and suggestive thigh massages. It was just before ten when he paid the bill and walked Francine to her car in the parking lot.

Without warning, she turned and wound her arms around his neck, pressing her breasts flush against his chest. Then she kissed him, pushing her tongue inside his mouth, where it sought out his in much the same way a piranha seeks out prey. It attacked.

And Cam felt…nothing.

Well, not quite nothing—he felt disappointed. *Hugely* disappointed. True, Francine wasn't his type, but he'd expected to feel something, if only to prove that his reaction to Maddie had been hormone-induced. But even with this woman whose very demeanor screamed sex, there'd been no low pull in his stomach, no flutter in his chest.

When the kiss ended, Francine nipped his earlobe and whispered, "I live on the East Bay, but it's not that far from here. Do you want directions or do you want to follow me?"

"Actually, I think I'll just say good-night here." He untwined her arms and stepped away from her. Maybe losing himself in the warm body of a willing woman would take the edge off this loneliness and the odd restlessness he'd felt since the Cherry Festival. But looking at Francine's overmade-up face, he knew having sex with her would be more sordid than satisfying.

"I had a good time," he lied.

"You haven't had anything yet, sugar. It's early. Come back to my place and I'll show you what a good time really is. My roommate is gone for the weekend, so we'll have the house all to ourselves." She stepped forward again, arms already reaching for him. Cam stepped away, and held up a hand that caused her overplucked eyebrows to pucker.

"I have to be going. But thanks again."

"You're saying no?" She rested a hand on one well-curved hip, clearly flabbergasted.

"Good night."

He thought he heard her swear something rather creative when he turned and walked to his truck.

Cam had no reason to rush home. Without Caroline there, his house would be dark and quiet, with little more than cloud-filtered moonlight and the chirp of crickets for company on what he already knew would be a sleepless night. He turned and cruised through downtown Traverse City, not paying any particular attention to where he was going until he noticed the True Love, Incorporated logo done up in neon pink. The lobby lights burned brightly even though a closed sign hung in the window. He pulled into the municipal parking lot just behind the building, oddly disappointed when he didn't see Maddie's car there.

But then he spied her through the open blinds at

the window to her office. She was seated at her desk, flipping through a file folder, a cup of what he assumed was coffee or some other caffeinated beverage at her elbow. Before he could change his mind, Cam parked his truck and walked to the window. Maddie started a bit at his tapping, but then her face brightened as recognition dawned. She motioned for him to go around to the front.

Maddie flipped the locks on the door and greeted Cameron with a smile. He looked troubled and more handsome than she liked to remember. He'd cut his hair; it no longer rode his collar, curling up a little at the ends. She found she rather missed those defiant little curls.

"This is a surprise." She gestured for him to come in, catching a whiff of cologne as he passed. It wasn't the heavy, designer stuff Ted had worn. It was spicy but subtle. "I thought you had a date tonight. Francine Lyons. Don't tell me she didn't show. She seemed very eager to meet you."

"Eager isn't the word for it," Maddie thought he mumbled as he followed her back to her office.

"I'm afraid all I can offer you is water or coffee. I drank the last can of cola an hour ago."

"That's okay. I'm fine." He glanced around the small office. "I'm surprised to find you here at this time of night. Especially on a Friday. No hot date?"

"No hot date. But why don't we talk about your date?" she evaded smoothly. "Have a seat and tell me what you thought of Francine."

"Her friends call her Francie," he mimicked in a high-pitched voice before he slumped heavily into the chair. Stretching one long leg out in front of him, he repeated, "What did I think of Francine? Well, let's see. I think I'm lucky not to have been eaten alive."

Maddie cleared her throat. "Um, care to clarify that for me a bit?"

He looked away, seeming to study the framed artwork that hung on her wall. "Dating has changed a lot since I last went out with a woman. I guess I didn't realize how much until tonight. Francine was very..."

"Forward?" Maddie offered, remembering the woman's provocative demeanor. Admittedly, it had given her pause to set up Cameron with such a woman, but otherwise she seemed to fit his specifications so perfectly, and precious few women in Maddie's database did.

He straightened in his chair and finally glanced in her direction. "Forward? Any more forward and the woman would have been horizontal."

Maddie couldn't stifle an unladylike snort of laughter. "I admit that Francine can come across as a little aggressive."

"She could give lessons to a barracuda," he added dryly.

She noticed that some of the tension had eased from his shoulders and he smiled now. Why was it when he smiled like that, she always felt a strange tightness in her chest, as if the oxygen were being squeezed from her lungs?

"That bad?"

"Let's just put it this way, the only kind of hit in her game was a home run. I prefer to work my way around the bases at my own pace."

Maddie hoped she wasn't blushing, but she was pretty sure she was. She remembered that sweet, blissful kiss they'd shared and, continuing his baseball metaphor, wondered if that was how he warmed up for a big game. Her cheeks grew even warmer. To cover her consternation, she said, "Why don't we revisit your date preferences. Perhaps I missed something."

"Nah." He waved a hand and sighed. "I don't think it was your fault. It was mine. She *was* a perfect match based on what I described as my type of woman, but Francine Lyons and women like her are not what I'm looking for."

"Then perhaps we should go over again what it is that you're looking for."

"I keep telling you and everyone else that I'm not looking at all."

"But if you were?" she persisted.

"Someone like Angie, I guess," he said softly. She noticed he glanced at his left hand. No wedding band encircled his ring finger, but Maddie knew he felt its weight there, even so.

As if he read her thoughts, he dug into one of the front pockets of his jeans and produced the ring in question. He stared at it for a moment before finally slipping it back onto his finger, and she swore she heard him sigh.

He glanced up, as if daring her to comment. Instead, she asked, "What was she like?"

"What was Angie like?" He expelled a deep breath. "Smart, sexy, funny. She could make me laugh at the oddest times. We'd be in a fight over finances or some other stupid thing. I'd be yelling and slamming cupboard doors.'' He sent Maddie a lopsided grin and shrugged. ''That's kinda my specialty. Then, she'd say, 'I think you should slam that one again, Cam, the dishes barely rattled. On a scale of one to ten, that slam barely rated a five. You can do better.''' He chuckled softly at the memory. ''She made me feel so ridiculous that I couldn't help but laugh. Then we'd both be laughing and...''

''And making up?'' Maddie finished for him.

He nodded. ''I never could stay mad at Angie for long. She made it impossible.''

''I'd like to hear more about her, if you're willing to share it.''

It wasn't professional curiosity that prompted her to ask. She thought talking about his late wife might be a comfort to Cameron. Maddie knew from experience that even close friends often shied away from broaching painful subjects. Few of her friends ever brought up the loss of her unborn son—even her own family avoided the topic. But Maddie wanted to talk about it, needed to. Perhaps Cameron did as well.

''How did you meet?''

''At a dinner put on by one of the other cherry farmers. My folks were still running the orchard then and they made me tag along. I didn't want to go. Complained bitterly about it all the way there. Then I walked in and saw her. She had on this white dress that seemed to float around her. She looked like an angel. Later in the evening, when the men started grousing about crop prices, she rolled her eyes at me and mouthed, 'Meet me outside.' I did. We shared a piece of cherry pie—ate it off the same fork. I didn't kiss her that night, but I wanted to. I was hooked.''

''She must have been special.''

''She was.''

''You obviously loved her deeply. I envy you that, Cameron.'' In a soft voice, Maddie admitted, ''I've never known that kind of love.''

''Then why did you marry that Ted character?''

She picked nonexistent lint from the sleeve of her blouse. Her tone was rueful when she said, ''Well, my mother liked him. It was the first time she'd liked anyone I'd brought home. I guess I took that as some sort of sign.''

''Come on, Maddie. That can't be the only reason.''

''No, it's not. I thought I loved him, and I thought he loved me. It seemed right. I wanted to be a wife. I wanted children, a family.''

''He must have wanted children, too, judging from his new bride's condition.''

''Oh, Ted wanted children. More than anything,'' she whispered. Far more, it had turned out, than he'd wanted Maddie for a wife, not that she particularly blamed him given what had happened.

Before the silence could grow too awkward, Cam stood. ''Well, I guess I should be going. Caroline is at Eve's for the night, but I promised to call her if I returned home before it got too late.''

She walked with him to the door, sliding open the dead bolts. Before he could leave, she placed a hand on his arm.

"So, do you want to try again? I'll try to find someone more suited to your tastes this time."

He glanced out at the street and shrugged. "Why not? I don't plan to let you win our bet by default."

"Cam, let's forget about the bet."

He leaned against the doorjamb and offered a lazy grin. "Well, well. I was wondering if you'd ever do it."

Maddie felt as if she'd just touched an exposed electrical wire. The current surged through her, seeming to set every atom of her being into motion.

"D-do it?" she stammered.

"Call me Cam instead of Cameron." He watched her face flush, noted the way she clasped and unclasped her hands, and he found himself rather enjoying the fact that he could so easily fluster her.

"You said that's what your friends call you. I'd like to think we've become friends." She offered a tentative smile, made all the more poignant because of its rareness.

"We're friends, Maddie," he confirmed.

Without thinking, he reached out to tuck a dark curl behind her ear, and then he stroked a finger down her cheek. Her skin was soft, her makeup so minimal that it didn't hide or compete with her natural beauty. He watched the pulse thrum at the base of her throat. Her eyes were wide and wary.

He didn't plan to kiss her, like the last time, it just happened. He leaned forward, and their lips met once, twice. But the friendly touch of mouths was not enough. He stepped closer, invading her personal space, although she didn't seem to mind. He thought he heard her draw in a breath just as, seemingly of their own volition, his fingers weaved through the mass of mahogany hair that framed her face.

This kiss was openmouthed and deep. It wasn't about desire, but about need. The need to satisfy his curiosity, to feel again, to discover. And discover, he did. He discovered that Maddie Daniels fit quite nicely in the circle of his arms. He discovered that he liked the way her breasts pressed against his chest. He discovered he liked the light, seductive scent of her perfume and the way her delicate hands first skimmed and then clutched his shoulders as if she had to hold on tight just to remain upright.

He hadn't imagined the intensity of that first kiss, after all, Cam realized, and he definitely wasn't prepared for the searing heat of this one. But as deep and erotic as the kiss was, Cam wanted more. His hands moved down her slim torso and rested momentarily at her waist, then he boldly stroked her hips, urging her body closer until there could be no mistake about his interest.

A low moan jolted him back to reality. He wasn't sure who had issued it, just as he wasn't sure who was more shocked by his actions. He stumbled back a step, and his shoulder glanced off the doorjamb.

He thought about Francine Lyons and the way she had fastened her eager, red-painted mouth over his. After that kiss he'd felt disappointed, and lonelier than ever. He'd convinced himself that no one could ever cause the same kind of physical reaction he'd enjoyed with Angela. He'd convinced himself that he hadn't really felt that blast of heat when he'd kissed

Maddie at the Cherry Festival, but there was no denying his jumping pulse or aroused state now.

The guilt came as quickly as a prizefighter's fist. How could he feel this way about another woman? Hadn't he loved his wife? He pushed out the door, ashamed of his actions, ashamed of the desire that had yet to recede.

Walking backward a few steps, he said, "That was wrong. All wrong. I don't want you."

The words came out in an angry staccato, while Maddie just stood there, lips rosy and slightly parted, eyes glazed with the same desire that mocked him. He turned and left—fled was more like it—before she could utter a single syllable.

In the parking lot, Cam sat in his truck and sucked in several deep, calming breaths. They didn't help. There was no denying it this time—his libido, permanently reawakened from its long hibernation, was humming along in overdrive. He caught a glimpse of Maddie through her office window as she sat at her desk. She brushed something from her cheek. Tears, he realized. The tears of a woman who had just been ill-used and then thoughtlessly rejected.

"I'm so sorry," he whispered into the darkness. But he wasn't sure to which woman he was apologizing—Maddie Daniels or his dead wife.

Chapter Six

Maddie stumbled to her desk, then sat. She stared at the paperwork before her, determined to work, but it blurred hopelessly with her tears. She swiped them away, mindless of what that might do to the meager amount of mascara she wore, but more tears followed stubbornly on their heels.

Cameron doesn't want me.

She squeezed her eyes shut, hearing again the anger and accusation in his tone. Of course, he wouldn't want someone like her. She'd been a fool to think, even for that one out-of-control moment, that he might. But what man would, especially if he could see the entirety of her scarred body, or knew the full truth about her personal failings?

She thought she had accepted that she would pass the rest of her life alone. That finding a special someone for other people was as close as she deserved to come to experiencing such excitement herself. But as she traced a finger over her lips, Maddie knew it would be harder now to sit on life's sidelines. The kiss had packed the quick heat of a blowtorch and had allowed, just for an instant, hope to rise blindly from the ashes of her past. But some things could not be resurrected. Maddie knew this better than anyone.

Three weeks passed before Maddie worked up the nerve to contact Cameron. She had needed the time and the distance to get her thoughts in order before facing him again, even over the telephone. The brilliant plan she'd come up with was to pretend that the interlude in her office hadn't happened. Barring that, she would treat it as the unrepeatable mistake Cameron considered it, for that's all it had been. Cameron was lonely, and he'd been out of sorts after his disastrous first date. As for Maddie, she couldn't find an excuse.

What she did find, however, was another date for Cameron. Before dialing his number, she flipped open the file and stared at the black-and-white photograph. The face that stared back was lovely, and nothing at all like Cameron's description of his ideal woman, but Maddie had gone on instinct in picking pretty Peggy Modean. The woman was slim and petite with a short cap of dark hair and an acre-wide smile. She was a real estate agent by trade, and a little closer to thirty than she was to twenty-five, but her diminutive stature and pixie features made her look barely old enough to drive.

Peggy liked kids, even volunteered at Munson Medical Center in the children's ward. She could play a baby grand with the training of a concert pianist, but she preferred banging out up-tempo tunes on a battered upright during open-mike night at the Patty James Pub. She had a lovely voice, melodious even in speech. She was an attentive listener, an avid sports fan and her sense of humor leaned toward the ridiculous. She liked *The Three Stooges,* for heaven's sake. What man could resist a woman who could tolerate that bumbling trio?

Peggy knew wine, and enjoyed traveling to vineyards both in the United States and abroad. Still, she liked beer, cold and frothy, when she attended a Tigers game. And while Detroit might be two hundred and fifty miles to the south, she hadn't missed an opening day in seven years.

Maddie sighed. She just knew Peggy and Cameron would hit it off wonderfully. The woman had second-date material stamped all over her perky face.

With that thought, she promptly hung up the phone. Pretty Peggy could wait. Maddie had until February to win the bet, after all. Between now and then there were all sorts of women Cam might enjoy meeting— once. He needed to get his feet back under him, Maddie rationalized. He shouldn't be forced to dive right into a relationship. Satisfied that she was doing this for his own good, she shuffled through the files on her desk. Finding what she was looking for, she picked up the telephone again and dialed.

"Foley residence."

"Hello, Mrs. Haversham. This is Maddie Daniels. I would like to leave a message for Cameron, please."

It was nearly noon, so she didn't expect to find him at home.

"No need to leave a message," the housekeeper replied. "He's right here."

Maddie's heart skipped several beats when the rich, deep timbre of Cameron's voice greeted her. She was grateful he couldn't see her, because she was sure she was blushing, as the remembered heat from that last kiss flooded her cheeks.

"Hello, Cameron."

"Back to Cameron, I see." He sounded almost grim.

The reference, discreet as it was, to that night in her office threw Maddie off balance. She'd assumed he'd be as eager as she to pretend it had never occurred.

"Um, I..."

"I think we need to talk," he interrupted quietly.

She chose to ignore his suggestion. "I've been busy going through my database and I've found someone I think you'll enjoy meeting."

There was a snort of disbelief, followed by silence.

"Her name is Leta Reveaux and she recently relocated to Traverse City from Buffalo, but she was born and raised in nearby Benzie County, so she's really a local girl at heart. Her grandparents even dabbled in cherries, so you have that in common. Of course, their operation was nothing on the scale of your farm, but she spent enough summers there to know the difference between a Montmorency and a Schmidt." Maddie proudly rattled off the names of two varieties of cherry, one tart and the other sweet, that she'd looked up on an Internet site.

"Now, that's just what I look for in a woman," he remarked dryly. "But if I put a cherry pit under a pile of mattresses will she be able to sleep?"

She pretended not to hear the sarcasm. "So, are you interested?"

Harsh laughter greeted her question. "Am I interested? Maddie, we need to—"

"When do you have a free night?" she interrupted.

Cam wanted to talk to Maddie. At the very least, he figured he owed her an apology for coming on to her that way in her office, and then bumbling the situation so badly afterward. He'd picked up the telephone a dozen times during the past few weeks, but always hung up before dialing her office number. Now she was on the other end of the line, offering to set him up on another date. He supposed he should be grateful she wasn't holding a grudge or acting aggrieved.

Yet, oddly enough, he wasn't.

"So, Cameron, when can you meet her?" she asked again.

Maddie was all business this day, so Cam decided to oblige her. He glanced at the calendar that hung on the wall next to the refrigerator. Might as well get it over with, he thought with a grimace, the memory of Francine Lyons still fresh enough to make him shudder.

"I guess I've got nothing going on this Saturday, if that's all right with her."

"Great. I'll give Leta a call and set something up,

and then I'll get back with you and let you know a time and place. Unless you have something in mind?''

"I'll yield to your expert judgment."

"Fine," she said, her tone annoyingly sunny. "I'll be in touch."

"Maddie!" he shouted into the receiver, afraid she was about to hang up. Mrs. Haversham shot him a curious glance as she prepared tuna-salad sandwiches for lunch.

"Yes, Cameron?"

Cam turned away from his housekeeper's prying eyes and lowered his voice to barely above a whisper, wishing he were on the cordless phone so that he could have the conversation in private. He settled on walking to the far end of the kitchen, stretching the curling cord until it was a straight white line, but of course it still fell one foot short of taking him into the screened-in porch.

"About that night in your office. I wanted to apologize for…for, well, you know."

"Cameron, there's no need to apologize."

Her voice was so formal, so proper and Southern-sounding, that he could all but taste the mint julep. Unless he was mistaken, she used that tone whenever she was ill at ease. Well, he was none to comfortable with the situation himself.

"Still, I'm a little embarrassed by my behavior. I've been meaning to call, but…"

But he hadn't known exactly what to say. *Sorry for mauling you? Sorry for being turned on by you?*

Sorry for feeling the first tingle of arousal I've experienced in three long and lonely years?

Sorry for hating you for making it happen?

"It's forgotten, really," she assured him before hanging up.

Forgotten? How nice for her that she was able to so easily push from memory the same kiss that had given him a dozen restless nights. It didn't matter, he told himself, as he sat down and began to eat his lunch, all but oblivious to his daughter's constant stream of chatter and Mrs. Haversham's well-meaning attempts at conversation. It was just wounded male pride that caused this huge ball of disappointment to weigh on his chest. He caught the glint of gold on his left hand. Wounded male pride and guilt.

It was just past ten o'clock on Saturday night, but Cam sat at his kitchen table, working a crossword puzzle and drinking a beer—his second since coming home an hour earlier. Date two had been a disaster. Oh, Leta Reveaux was nice enough and she'd kept her hands to herself. There had been no aggressive thigh massages, no bold invitations to carnal delight. She was more helpless kitten than sex-starved vixen.

They met at a restaurant that specialized in Mexican food. Cam loved anything spicy, but after watching Leta pop half a bottle of antacids, it became clear she didn't have the stomach lining for south-of-the-border fare. But she never complained. He got the feeling she never complained about anything. She listened attentively, even when he knew his desperate chatter about baseball would have bored a die-hard fan. But her small rosebud of a mouth had remained firmly shut, giving Cam the choice of either dominating the conversation or squirming in uncomfortable silence.

After a couple of hours in her company, his voice had turned almost raspy. Caroline could wash down an entire box of chocolates with a can of cola and not talk as much as he had during that interminably long dinner. It had been a relief to end the evening and come home. Maybe he just wasn't cut out for this dating business any longer.

His second beer was empty, and opening a third seemed mighty tempting. Caroline was tucked in for the night. Tomorrow he could sleep late before going to church. He twisted the cap off another long-necked brown bottle and, without stopping to wonder if she would be there, he punched in Maddie's office number. She answered on the fifth ring.

"How come I knew you would be there? You've got to get out more, *Miss Daniels.* You're becoming predictable."

"Cameron." He thought he heard a smile in her voice when she said his name. Perhaps it was for the best, he decided, that by unspoken agreement, they'd put that kiss business behind them.

"How are you, Maddie?"

"Fine. How's the evening going?"

"Not bad. But I'm stuck on twenty-three down. A nine-letter word starting with *P* that means concerned with facts."

"Pragmatic," she murmured before asking,

"You're working a crossword? What happened to Leta?"

"Miss Muffet and I parted ways a couple of hours ago."

"Okay, I give. Why are you calling her Miss Muffet?"

"'Cause if a spider had sat down beside her, it would have frightened her away."

"Leta is a bit shy. Was the evening all bad?"

He sighed, took a quick pull on his beer and paced the length of the kitchen. "I can't decide if dating has changed or if I have. Has it always been this hard?"

"I'm not the best person to ask," she admitted. "I didn't date much before I married Ted."

"And after your divorce?" he asked quietly, although he thought he knew the answer.

"Too busy finding dates for people like you. And obviously I'm not doing a very good job if you're working a crossword alone on a Saturday night."

He sat at the table and propped his feet on the chair opposite his. "I'm not working it alone."

"Oh, is Caroline still up?"

"No. The sitter somehow managed to have her in bed before I got home." Cradling the phone with his shoulder, he plucked the pen from the tabletop. "What's the opposite of *endo?* Four letters."

"Does it start with an *E?*"

"I don't know, but the second letter is a C."

"*Ecto.*"

"Hey, you're good at this," he replied, jotting down the answer.

"It's my one guilty pleasure. I work the crossword even before I read the newspaper."

"Your secret's safe with me. So, what's a nine-letter word for *starting point?* Ends in *G*."

"Hmm. Ends in *G?* Ah, that would be *beginning*."

Yes, Cam thought, an odd sort of acceptance settling in. Beginning.

Cam had another date. In fact, it was his third since Miss Muffet. Each had been slightly better than the last, although none had been terribly exciting. But he enjoyed the dates because afterward he always called Maddie, and they talked, sometimes for hours. This one was a bank manager with a fondness for Chinese.

He was due to meet Corey Carver at a restaurant in less than an hour, but nothing was going his way. He'd had an emergency in the orchard that had required his attention till late in the afternoon, and then he'd arrived at the house to news that his sitter had canceled for the evening. Mrs. Haversham couldn't stay, because Saturday was her euchre night with the ladies, and Eve and Richard had taken the boys to the Upper Peninsula for the long Labor Day weekend to see Lake Superior's impressive Pictured Rocks National Lakeshore. He had no choice but to postpone his date.

He dialed Maddie's office number. It saddened him to think that even though it was a holiday weekend and after five o'clock, she would be there, stuck behind her desk eating cold take-out and drinking something that contained a respectable jolt of caffeine.

She picked up on the third ring.

"Hey, Maddie. It's Cam."

"This is a surprise."

"Actually, this is bad news. I'm sorry for the short notice, but I'm afraid I'm going to have to call off my date for tonight. I was wondering how best to get in touch with Corey."

It was True Love, Incorporated's policy to set up the first date and then let the couple exchange numbers and addresses as they saw fit.

"Is something wrong?"

"Nothing serious. My sitter canceled at the last minute and I can't find anyone else to watch Caroline on such short notice on a Saturday night."

After only a slight pause, Maddie offered, "I can watch Caroline tonight."

"I can't ask you to do that."

"You didn't ask me, I volunteered. I'll call Corey and let her know you'll be late. Give me about half an hour. I need to close up here."

True to her word, Maddie wrapped things up at her office and arrived in less than thirty minutes. It had taken her longer than expected to reach Corey, so she'd had to drive a little faster than what usually made her comfortable. But she hadn't broken into a cold sweat this time, so she considered it progress.

The scenery had whirred by, but she'd actually enjoyed the drive. Coming home later that night would be a different story, she knew, already dreading it. She had avoided driving after dark since her accident. But she shook off her uneasiness and walked briskly to Cameron's front door. Caroline was on the big front porch, sitting at a small table having a tea party with her dolls.

"Daddy's in the house. He said to go on in, but you could come back out after you see him and have a cup of tea with us." She waved a small, chubby hand in the direction of the miniature empty chair directly across from hers.

Maddie sent her a gracious smile and turned her drawl especially thick when she replied, "Why, Miss Caroline, I can think of nothing I'd rather do than have tea with you. I'll be back shortly to partake of your hospitality."

Maddie entered the house without knocking, a serious faux pas in her mother's etiquette book. Instead, she stood in the foyer and called out Cameron's name to announce her arrival. She thought she heard a muffled greeting coming from somewhere down the hallway, so she started in that direction, calling out his name again.

Sure enough, he poked his head out of a doorway and motioned for her.

"Could you come here a minute and give me a hand?" he asked before disappearing again.

When she reached the room, he was seated on the edge of a big sleigh bed. Although they had spoken on the telephone regularly during the past several weeks, it was the first time she'd actually seen Cameron since that last kiss. And while being alone with him in his bedroom made her uneasy, it wasn't nearly as disturbing to her pulse as the fact that he wasn't wearing a shirt. She tried not to stare, but she couldn't help herself. Cameron Foley was hands-down the most gorgeous man she'd ever encountered. His muscled chest was as tanned as his face and dusted with dark hair, and his abdomen showed no ill effects from either his fondness for an occasional cold beer or his daughter's penchant for pizza. Maddie felt the saliva evaporate from her mouth.

"I'm in a bit of a dilemma," he admitted, sounding oddly chagrined and blessedly unaware of the direction of her thoughts.

"Dilemma?" she croaked. She needed to do something with her hands, so she settled on stuffing them into the pockets of her navy cotton trousers.

"I popped a button while I was dressing. No big deal, right? I mean, I might be a guy, but I know how to sew on a button. But then I..."

"You what?"

"I sewed my shirt together," he admitted with an embarrassed chuckle.

He held it up so Maddie could see the proof. The front of the shirt was indeed sewn shut at the fourth buttonhole. She tried to tuck away her grin but realized she wasn't quite successful when he said, "Go ahead and laugh, but this was my favorite shirt, and the only one Mrs. Haversham ironed before she left."

"Ah. So, you'd attempt sewing, but not ironing?" She glanced at the abused shirt again and nodded sagely, "But then, I guess you would know your strong suit, and the fire department thanks you."

"Smart aleck," he muttered. "Can you sew while I finish shaving? Or would you prefer to iron another shirt?"

"Ever hear of permanent press?" she groused

good-naturedly, glad to trade sexual tension for humor.

While Cam disappeared into the adjoining bathroom to finish getting ready, Maddie settled onto the edge of the mattress and opened the sewing box that sat on the nightstand. The box looked like a frilly treasure chest, all done up in a padded floral print. His late wife's, she decided, feeling a bit like an interloper when she reached inside and selected a pair of small scissors. She clipped the threads from Cameron's sloppy job and neatly sewed on the button. As she worked, she heard Cameron humming. The tune was slightly off key, but unmistakably vintage Bob Seger. She smiled and began to hum along. She liked Bob Seger, too.

"All done?"

Cameron stood in the doorway, hands gripping the ends of the blue-and-white-striped towel that hung around his neck. He looked as if he should be gracing the cover of some physical fitness magazine. Desire returned in a breath-stealing rush. Maddie hastily glanced away before she could gawk again.

"Just about."

She snipped the thread and somehow managed to tie it off with her shaking fingers.

"Here you are." She offered the shirt to him, determined to act professionally, even as her heart thudded in her chest and her pulse pounded out an erratic tattoo. And that was before he crossed to her, bringing with him the aroma of his cologne. She swore she'd smelled that subtle scent all night after the kiss in her office.

"Thanks, Maddie."

Just for a moment she allowed herself the fantasy that they were a couple, that this was their home, their bedroom, and that Cameron was her husband, her lover. Need curled inside her like smoke from a campfire, but her heart felt singed. Cameron may have kissed her. They may be friends. But he'd made it clear that he didn't want her. And she had no right to want him.

Cam shrugged into his shirt, trying not to feel self-conscious, but how could he not with Maddie sitting on his bed? She looked uncomfortable, nervous. And unaccountably sexy in her plain cotton slacks and prim long-sleeved blouse. He turned around so that he could unzip his pants and tuck in the tails of his shirt. The chivalrous gesture was wasted, he realized, when he glanced up to find her watching him in the large beveled mirror that hung over the dresser. Color stained her cheeks, and her gaze slid away, but not before he saw interest and awareness burning there.

He turned around slowly, took a step forward, even though he wasn't sure how to proceed. But he needed to touch her, wanted to taste her again. His fingers had barely skimmed her hair when Caroline skipped into the room wearing a full accoutrement of costume jewelry and a floppy straw hat. Cam was torn between annoyance and relief.

"Darling," his daughter drawled, tossing back one pigtail with all the flair of a debutante. The six strands of colored beads that hung around her neck tinkled noisily. "The tea is getting cold."

"I beg your pardon." Maddie transferred her gaze

to Cam and plastered a game grin on her face. Her voice was thick Southern honey when she announced, "Your daughter was kind enough to invite me to tea, and I've kept her waiting long enough. Please excuse us."

Cam watched them go. The girl playing dress-up, the woman playing it cool.

Fifteen minutes later, Cam found them on the front porch, having a heart-to-heart chat about how they would redecorate Barbie's Dream House. Caroline was pouring a make-believe cup of tea. Maddie, a rather silly-looking hat perched atop her head, was folded up like a piece of origami on one of his daughter's small chairs. They made quite the picture.

"Are you ladies enjoying yourselves?"

"We're having a simply delightful time," Caroline informed him grandly, then took a sip of her pretend tea.

It still amazed him when she used big words in the right context. He dropped a kiss on his daughter's nose and admonished lightly, "You be good for Maddie, and don't try to weasel her into letting you stay up past your bedtime."

Maddie braced herself on the table and rose as gracefully as possible from her seat. It surprised him that, given her particular physical limitations, she would attempt to sit on such a short stool in the first place. But then she seemed to have a genuine liking for children in general, and his daughter in particular.

"Emergency numbers and the one for my cell

phone are posted on the refrigerator. If you need anything, just call me."

"We'll be fine," she assured him.

Yes, but Cam wondered if he would be. It seemed odd to be leaving to spend the evening with another woman when two of his favorite females were right here. That little revelation had him taking a hasty step backward. Oh, he liked Maddie, all right. And, although he still wasn't sure how he felt about it, he was drawn to her physically. But enjoying someone's company and fantasizing about having sex with her was vastly different from wanting her in your home. Often.

When exactly had Maddie wormed her way so neatly into his life that the idea of spending an evening in the company of another attractive woman seemed a little too much like a consolation prize?

"Uh, you guys can order pizza if you want. I left some money on the kitchen countertop. Or you can heat up the leftover lasagna that's in the fridge. I won't be too late."

Maddie smiled. Was it his imagination, or did she look almost sad when she said, "I hope you have a good time, Cameron."

Maddie watched until Cam's truck had disappeared from sight. She might have kept staring down the dusty road had Caroline not collapsed onto the porch in a tinkle of beads and, drawing a hand across her brow, announced dramatically, "I'm starving to death."

"Well, which will it be? Leftover lasagna or pizza?"

"Pizza!" Caroline squealed.

"I was hoping you'd say that." Maddie grinned. "Please tell me you like pepperoni."

An hour and a half later, Maddie was wrapping the remains of their pizza in tinfoil when Caroline trudged into the kitchen wearing her pajamas and dragging an abused-looking teddy bear by one of its raggedy ears.

"Okay, I'm ready for bed. You said we could watch my favorite video before I have to go to sleep."

"So I did," Maddie replied with a nod. "Did you remember to brush your teeth?"

The child offered a gap-toothed grin. "Yep."

"Well, then, let's go watch that video."

Maddie put in the video and sat on the couch, surprised but touched when Caroline crawled trustingly onto her lap.

"There's a couple of scary parts," the girl said soberly. "The beast sometimes roars and shows his fangs. But he has a good heart. That's what my daddy always tells me. He says that sometimes people act nasty only 'ause they're scared or lonely or no one taught them any better."

"Your daddy's a smart man," Maddie replied, giving the child a quick hug. She smelled like strawberries thanks to a quick bubble bath, and Maddie took a moment to imagine what her son would have been like—what her life would have been like—had the accident not occurred and changed everything. She wouldn't own a dating service, that went without saying. Ted wouldn't have stood for her working at all.

Ted. She would still be married to him. She would still be living in the lavishly furnished house downstate, a suburban housewife and mother driving a minivan and volunteering at only those charities his mother deemed acceptable. Her son would have been the much-anticipated heir to an old-money fortune. She frowned. Except for Michael, she didn't miss the rest of it.

Caroline snapped a finger in front of her face.

"Oh, Maaad-die. Earth to Maddie," she sang out in her squeaky six-year-old voice.

"Sorry, daydreaming."

"My daddy does that sometimes. And he looks sad like you just did, too. I think he still misses my mommy. She's in heaven, you know."

"That's right."

"I used to hear my daddy crying at night when he thought I was asleep, but he doesn't cry anymore."

Maddie's heart twisted. "He loved your mom very much. That kind of love is especially rare. It's called true love."

"Kinda like your business," Caroline chirped, looking pleased with herself. "True Love, Incorperlated. Are you going to find him another true love?"

"I don't know if I can do that, but maybe I'll find him someone he'll enjoy spending time with."

"Then your job is done," Caroline said thoughtfully.

"Why do you say that?"

The child grinned knowingly. "My daddy enjoys spending time with you."

Well past midnight, Cam pulled his truck to a halt in front of the garage and hopped out. He tilted back his head, scanning the inky expanse of sky. It was a clear night and the heavens seemed to hold a million stars. He spied the Big Dipper and smiled. Despite a course in astronomy in college, it was still the only constellation he could readily pick out.

Jogging up the walk, he drew in a deep breath. The cool evening air carried the scent of juniper and the white pines that lined his property at the road. It had been a long time since he'd enjoyed the simple pleasures of a country night. During the day, his cherry trees gave him enough to contemplate. But for the past three years, the nights had been a time of recriminations and second-guessing. Should they have tried other cancer specialists? Should he have insisted they journey to Mexico for that unorthodox treatment he'd read about on the Internet? Angie had been firm in her refusal, but what if...?

This night seemed different, filled with more anticipation than anguish.

The lights were on when he entered, but the house was quiet. He found Maddie on the couch, slumped sideways as if she had tried to wait up for him, but dreams had beckoned. He got the feeling that she didn't get the recommended eight hours. She looked younger in sleep. Younger and more vulnerable. The scarred hand was tucked beneath her head on the couch cushion, and the way she was positioned, he knew she would be stiff when she awoke.

Gently, he shook her shoulder. She came awake slowly, a little disoriented at first, he decided, when she smiled at him in a sleepy, sexy way that had him swallowing hard.

"Cameron, you're home." She sat up, brushed the hair back from her face and smoothed the wrinkles from her clothes.

"I just got in." He consulted his watch. "It's twelve-thirty."

"Sorry, I fell asleep." She stifled a yawn.

"No need to apologize. How about a cup of coffee to help you wake up before you head out?"

Maddie seemed to tense, but she smiled when she replied, "Coffee would be great."

They drank their coffee on the porch. It seemed too nice of a night to be cooped up indoors, and Cam had missed sitting on the porch swing with another adult, discussing the day's events while being serenaded by the chirp of crickets and tree frogs and the occasional hoot of an owl.

Maddie sipped her coffee. It was strong and black and she could already feel the caffeine revving up her sluggish system.

"It's a pretty night," she commented.

"Yeah, but a little cool." He glanced in her direction. "Are you sure you don't need a sweater?"

Maddie curled her hands around the warm mug. "I'm fine. The night air should help wake me up. So, what did you think of Corey? You weren't back by ten, so that's a good sign."

She studied his profile while she awaited a response. He had a strong jaw, more often clenched than not, but she'd glimpsed tenderness there. She'd seen vulnerability.

"Corey is nice. We had a good time."

The benign adjectives made her absurdly happy. Still, she held her breath when she asked, "Is there a date two in your future?"

Cam thought about it for a moment. Under normal circumstances, he might have considered Corey second-date material. She *was* nice, not to mention easy on the eye. But for a good portion of the evening, he'd found himself preoccupied with what Maddie and Caroline were up to at home. If he had a second date with Corey, he probably wouldn't see Maddie again or at least not very often. The terms of their bargain would be met. He found he didn't want to let her out of his life—at least not until he figured out exactly why he felt so compelled to keep her in it.

"Nah," he said with a casual lift of his shoulders. "I want to leave my options open."

They sat in companionable silence for a few minutes before Cam confided, "I miss this."

"What?"

"Sitting on a porch swing at night. Angie and I used to do it all the time."

"What else do you miss?" she asked quietly.

He didn't plan to answer. He planned to change the subject with some smart-alecky retort, but he heard himself admit, "I miss seeing another toothbrush next to mine in the holder, and I miss having someone to share my first cup of coffee with in the morning."

Silence greeted his words and Cam laughed harshly. "That probably sounds stupid, huh?"

"Not at all. People tend to think those who have lost loved ones only feel bad around the holidays, but just as life is about the little things, so is grief. Sometimes it's the mundane, day-to-day stuff that can be the hardest to endure."

He thought about that for a moment, appreciating Maddie's practical nature and the way she invited confidences. No one else seemed to want to hear these things. No one except Eve even spoke Angie's name aloud. His friends' well-intentioned silence made it seem as if, worse than having died, Angie had never existed.

He felt Maddie take his hand, and the simple gesture set free the words he hadn't even realized had been trapped inside him.

"Do you know what I miss most of all?"

"Tell me."

"I miss having someone else to share my delight in Caroline's antics, my pride in her achievements, my heartache when I have to dole out discipline and I'm wondering, is it too much? Not enough? Sometimes I lie in bed at night and I worry that I'm not doing this parenting thing right. I mean, is she going to turn out okay?"

"Oh, Cameron." Maddie raised his hand to her lips, kissed the back of it before resting it against her cheek. "You're a wonderful father. Caroline is lucky to have you. She's going to be fine and so are you."

Cam nodded, and then made his most painful confession. "To tell you the truth, I can't always remem-

ber Angie. I mean, I remember the feelings, but sometimes I can't recall how her voice sounded or what
her hair felt like.''

''That doesn't make you a bad person. Grief has
stages. Denial, anger and so on. This is another stage.
It just means you're healing.''

While the swing swayed and the stars winked, Cam
considered her words. He appreciated the thoughtful
care with which Maddie offered them, just as, at long
last, he accepted their simple truth.

He put his arm around Maddie's shoulder, enjoying
the way she felt snuggled up against him there in the
darkness.

''Healing,'' he murmured.

And the idea of moving on no longer seemed quite
so wrong or quite so scary.

Chapter Seven

The first ribbons of light were beginning to uncurl in the eastern sky when Maddie left. Cam walked her to her car. He had done the same thing for his date just hours earlier, but where Cam had left Corey with a simple handshake, something a little friendlier seemed in order now. At first, the embrace was hesitant and oddly awkward, especially considering the passion that had sparked between them in the past. But Maddie hugged him back, resting her head on his shoulder. She sighed out his name in three soft syllables and he could feel her fine-boned hands patting his back. The gesture was one of comfort, but what he experienced was far more primal than that. How long had it been since a woman had simply hugged him and he'd felt this worked up?

"I can't believe we talked all night," he commented for lack of anything better to say when the hug ended. He moved a safe step back. "How sore are you from sitting on that swing?"

"I'm fine," she replied, but the rigid way she held herself told him it was a lie. He raised his hands and began to knead her shoulders. The muscles tensed briefly before he felt them begin to uncoil beneath his intent fingertips.

"Relax," he ordered, and, as if she was attempting to do just that, her eyelids fluttered shut, that quirky mole dipping. One side of her mouth curled up. The kiss he dropped onto it was light and friendly, but it had her eyelids flicking open just the same.

"I'd better go."

He only nodded. Why was it he wanted to urge her to stay?

"Well, good night, Cameron."

"It's morning, Maddie."

She laughed softly. "So it is."

"Thank you."

"You're welcome. I didn't mind watching Caroline."

"That's not what I meant." Showing enough restraint to qualify him for sainthood, he dropped another light kiss on her brow before opening the car door and helping her inside. "Drive safe."

"That I will."

As he went inside to snatch what sleep he could before Caroline bounded out of bed, Cam couldn't remember the last time he'd felt this peaceful, this cleansed of sorrow. Or, he admitted, this full of hope.

A distinct pattern developed in the weeks that followed. Maddie and Cam talked every day. Each night he called her at the office after Caroline had gone to bed. Each morning she reached him before he headed out the door to work in the orchard. This morning was no exception.

She heard him sipping his coffee on the other end of the line as they chatted. When she called in the mornings, they usually shared their first cup of coffee together. It hadn't been a conscious decision. Maddie hadn't really thought about Cameron's painful admission of missing someone to have morning coffee with when she'd made that first call, steaming mug in hand. It had just happened that way—and kept happening that way.

"How's your java this morning?" she asked, running a fingertip over the rim of the mug that sat on her desk blotter. She knew she probably had a goofy grin on her face. She was just grateful her observant receptionist wasn't there to see it and, like, smirk over it.

"Pretty good. Mrs. H. is getting better at grinding the beans so the coffee is neither bitter nor bland."

"I buy mine already ground. Saves time."

"Some things are meant to take a while," he said softly. "All that waiting makes them even better."

"Ah, anticipation."

"Yeah, it's more than a song title, you know."

"I know."

"Do you?" he asked, and Maddie got the feeling they were no longer talking about beans.

To file the dangerously flirtatious edge from the conversation, she fell back on humor. "Sure. It's also the answer to number twelve down in today's cross-word puzzle.''

"You need to get out more," he sighed. His tone was no longer teasing when he added, "I mean it, Maddie. You practically live in your office."

"I like my job."

"I like mine, too, but it's not the whole of my existence."

That stung, but it didn't make her as panicky as when he asked point-blank, "What's driving you?"

Maybe it was time to tell him. Maybe it was time to admit the one thing that Maddie considered more repulsive than her scars. "I..."

The light for the other extension flicked on then, and she gladly embraced the reprieve.

"Sorry, Cameron, but I've got to go. I've got a call on the other line. Maybe it's a new client." With forced brightness, she added, "Who knows, this one may even turn out to be the one for you."

Maddie nearly dropped the receiver when, after switching to the other line, she heard her mother's voice. Eliza Daniels never called her daughter at the office. She preferred not to acknowledge what Maddie did for a living, as she considered it a "tacky" vocation.

"This is a surprise, Mother. I hope everyone is fine."

"Yes, of course," Eliza returned politely, but Maddie got the feeling her mother was all but bursting at the seams to say something. Being Eliza Daniels, though, she padded the conversation with the requisite small talk for the next five minutes before finally getting around to the real reason for her call.

"I thought you would want to know that when we were leaving church on Sunday, Beau Richardson asked after you. I was thinking that perhaps we should invite him to supper the next time you come home."

Apparently matchmaking was not gauche as long as one didn't get paid for doing it. Maddie might have found humor in that thought had her mother's suggestion not caught her completely off guard.

"Beau? Isn't he a little young for me? If I recall right, he just graduated from high school last year."

Her mother chuckled delicately. "Good heavens, dear. I'm not talking about *young* Beau. I'm referring to his father."

"*Old* Beau?" Maddie sputtered, incredulous.

"Beau senior," Eliza corrected her. "He's been without a wife for six years now."

He was divorced, but it wasn't in her mother's vocabulary to say so, which made Maddie wonder how Eliza explained her daughter's single status to friends.

"He's a good man. Respectable, owns his own business." Eliza ticked off the man's attributes as if he were a used car she was trying to talk Maddie into buying.

"Mother, he's sixty if he's a day."

"Fifty-four, dear. Mature."

"Yes, mature enough to be my father."

Eliza sighed dramatically, her patience clearly worn thin. "I would think a woman in your situation would welcome the attention of such a successful man, older or not."

Maddie's head snapped back. She felt the slap coming all the way from Georgia.

"What situation would that be, Mother?" Perversely, she wanted to make her say it out loud, but Eliza Daniels excelled in the social graces. She was simply too good at avoiding unpleasantness to accommodate Maddie.

"You're so prickly," she chided. "That's not an especially appealing trait, dear."

"I'm just trying to figure out what makes me so pitiful that you think I should be thankful a man—any man—is interested in me. Is it the fact that I'm pushing thirty and divorced? Or that I'm permanently disfigured? Or is it that I'm unable to have children?"

"Madison, really. You're overwrought. I was just passing along a suggestion, that's all. You've blown this way out of proportion."

Maddie closed her eyes, kneaded her forehead. Her mother was right, and besides, it didn't matter. After what had happened, she would never marry again. She slipped into the well-remembered role of contrite daughter.

"I'm sorry. I didn't mean to snap your head off."

She very nearly snatched back the apology when her mother added, "That's all right, dear. But, you know, Beau doesn't want more children. His are grown and practically to the point of starting families themselves."

"I've got to go. Another call," Maddie said. Both women knew it was a lie. But then as long as you were polite, that made all sorts of things okay in Eliza Daniels's etiquette book.

Maddie hung up and tried to work, but her mother's words came back to her time and again. Nothing Eliza said had come as a surprise, although her words had unintentionally underscored the truth: Maddie would never remarry. She would spend her life alone, with no husband to love, no children to raise and nurture.

Why did that seem so much harder to accept now?

Fall arrived. All around the bay, maples and oaks blazed red and orange, while assorted other trees had turned as yellow as the sun. It was their last hurrah, one final and grand rush of glory before meeting their fate. Maddie walked along a paved trail that snaked along the waterfront near downtown. The change in weather had her leg stiff, which was why she'd decided to take a long walk. She'd brought her cane just in case, but was pleased that so far she didn't seem to be relying on it. The physical therapists had told her if she worked her leg muscles regularly, eventually she might not need the cane, even for longer distances.

As she walked the paved path, she nodded a greeting to the joggers and skaters she passed. Many of them wore headphones, listening to favorite songs as they went, but Maddie preferred nature's music. The breeze had waves breaking on the sand. Overhead, the gulls chattered noisily and swooped down like drunken pilots from the blue sky. While dark clouds loomed on the horizon, whatever foul weather might be brewing was too far off to dim her spirits on this perfect autumn afternoon.

"Hey, Maddie!" She turned to see Caroline and

Cameron zipping up behind her on in-line skates. She envied their agility and their skill. Even before her accident, she doubted she would have had the coordination or the confidence necessary to keep from breaking bones.

"Hey, yourself," she called back.

She allowed herself the most improper pleasure of admiring the way Cameron's well-worn jeans hugged his thighs as he glided toward her. His legs pumped rhythmically, even as her heartbeat became erratic. She noted with feminine satisfaction that his hair had grown out some so that the ends curled up slightly around the bottom of the National Cherry Festival ball cap he wore. She liked it better that way. He looked a little reckless and slightly dangerous compared to his daughter, who wore a jazzy purple-and-aqua helmet, a single ponytail tumbling out the back.

Caroline stopped by running into Maddie, nearly knocking her flat. Then she gripped Maddie's waist for support, although Maddie wasn't quite sure who was supporting whom for the moment it took to regain her balance.

"Sorry," Caroline mumbled contritely. "I haven't got the braking part down yet."

"You okay?" Cameron asked when he reached them. He gave Maddie's arm a friendly pat that sent her pulse on a ridiculously wild ride.

"Better than okay now," she said softly.

She couldn't believe she'd said the words aloud. Thinking them was foolish enough. But that didn't negate their truth. She'd been enjoying her peaceful, quiet walk, admiring nature's handiwork, but her whole world had brightened, broadened, shifted and filled when Cameron and Caroline skated into it. Old desires bubbled to the surface before she could cap the place in her heart that refused to accept that a husband and children would never be part of her future. Still, it felt good to pretend and, even briefly, to give in to old longings. Wasn't she entitled, every now and then, to want and to wish for the very things most women took for granted? She shifted the cane to her other hand so she could wrap an arm around Caroline. Squeezing the child to her side, she sent a smile in Cameron's direction.

"It's a great day, isn't it?" And she meant it. In that one moment, all was right with the world.

"Great day," Cam repeated, studying Maddie. Something about her was different today. Or rather, something had been changing for weeks now. She appeared happier, less guarded. She seemed to have shed some of that quiet sadness she'd worn like a heavy cloak when he'd first met her.

"We were coming to see you," he said. "We parked a few blocks away and planned to skate to your office."

"Really?"

"Uh-huh," Caroline added. "Daddy said if we didn't rescue you, you'd just sit in your office all day, kinda like Rapunzel in her tower, except your hair is dark and not quite as long."

"So, you were coming to rescue me? I like the sound of that. What were you going to do with me afterward?"

''We were all going to live happily ever after,'' the child replied with an emphatic nod.

''Actually, we were thinking about taking you to Clinch Park Zoo,'' Cam amended, although the happily-ever-after part didn't sound bad. Perhaps that's why he jumped when his beeper went off. He pulled it from the waistband of his jeans, noted the orchard number and sighed.

''Well, kiddo, it doesn't look like we'll be doing much rescuing today. I've got some work to do after all.'' To Maddie he said, ''I've been waiting for a part to come for one of the machines. Apparently it finally did.''

''Aw, Daddy, you promised me the whole afternoon.''

''I know. Next time.''

''I could take Caroline to the zoo, if…if that's all right with you,'' Maddie offered. ''Afterward, I could drive her home.''

He hesitated, but then he thought an afternoon at the zoo might be just what Maddie needed. He had a feeling if he said no, she would just walk back to her office and stay there well past the time most people were tucked in for the night.

''Can I stay with Maddie? Pleeease.''

Cam tweaked Caroline's upturned nose. ''Well, it looks like I'm outnumbered.'' Turning his attention to Maddie he added, ''I have one condition, though.''

''Of course.''

''You'll stay for dinner.''

''I think I can agree to that condition.''

She had worn her hair loose and the breeze tugged

at it, pulling dark ribbons of it across her cheek. He reached out and tucked what he could behind her ear. He meant it when he said, "I'm glad."

Maddie and Caroline sang on the drive back to the orchard, silly songs that the little girl made up and belted out unabashedly in her squeaky six-year-old voice. Maddie repeated an equally silly chorus at similar volume, even as her knuckles turned white on the steering wheel and her foot eased up on the accelerator. A violent wind had pushed ashore the inky storm clouds that had hovered over Lake Michigan earlier in the day. Rain splashed across the car's windshield, making it all but impossible to see, even with the wipers slashing over the glass on high.

"Are we there?" Caroline asked, straightening in the back seat so she could look out the side window, and Maddie realized she'd slowed to almost a stop.

"No, not yet. Let's…let's keep singing, okay?"

"Are you scared, Maddie?"

"Not at all," she lied bravely. "It's just a rainstorm. The roads are wet, but if I go slow, we'll be fine."

Maddie's eyes stung from not blinking. She would be more careful this time, she vowed. She just had to pay closer attention, stay more alert. Even as she thought it, upsetting memories of her accident and its ugly aftermath swarmed close. Maddie tried to shoo them away by coaxing her small passenger into another refrain of their made-up lyrics. She joined in again, somehow managing to sing around the ball of fear wedged in her throat.

They were nearly to the turnoff that would take them to the orchard when Maddie saw a pair of bright headlights coming straight at her through the storm's dimness. It was so eerily similar to that other time that at first she thought she might be imagining it. Even so, icy panic had her yanking the steering wheel hard to the right. The other driver raced past with a blast of his horn, while her car swerved onto the shoulder, skidding briefly on the gravel before coming to a jerky halt. Maddie's fingers loosened on the wheel, and she was just about to release the breath she'd been holding when the Volvo bucked violently. Caroline screamed. Or maybe, Maddie thought, it was she who had issued that high, keening wail.

"Are you all right?" Maddie called over her shoulder. Clumsy hands tried unsuccessfully three times to undo the safety belt that had her harnessed to the seat.

"I'm okay." But the little girl's voice hitched. "What happened?"

"Someone hit us from behind when we stopped. But we're okay. We're fine. We're fine," Maddie repeated like a mantra, trying to make herself believe it, trying to keep from slipping into that nightmare from the past.

A man appeared at her window, his face all but obscured by the rain slicker he wore. He tapped and motioned for Maddie to roll down her window. She opened it a crack, even as she depressed the locks. She'd read about people who rammed their cars into others, usually driven by women, and then victimized those people further. She was taking no chances, especially with Caroline in the car.

I will protect this child. I won't fail again.

The man pushed back the slicker a bit and she could see that he appeared harmless and a little shaken himself. She guessed him to be mid-forties, probably a fudgie on his way to the Indian-run casino in Peshawbestown.

"Hey, sorry about that, but that jerk ran us both off the road. I was too busy swerving to stop in time to avoid you." He glanced into the back seat, noticed Caroline. "Is everybody okay?"

"We're fine."

He nodded once, looking relieved. "I called the police on my cell phone to report the accident. Someone should be here in a few minutes. I'm going to go back to my car and wait." He hesitated a moment before adding, "I messed up your bumper pretty good. Just glad that's all the damage that was done."

Maddie's hands were ice-cold and she was shaking violently by the time the sheriff's deputy finished taking her statement and handed her a card with his name and the accident report number on it. She watched the rain drip from his plastic-covered sheriff's-issue cap as he gave her instructions on how to get a copy of the report and submit it to her insurance company. She knew how to deal with insurance companies, she thought dully. She'd been doing it for more than a year. Her agent's number was on the speed dial on her telephone at the office.

"The car's drivable, ma'am," the deputy said politely. "So you can go now."

Maddie thanked him and rolled up her window. The car could be driven, but could she drive it?

"Can we go home now?" came the plaintive cry from the back seat.

Maddie glanced in the rearview mirror and noted that Caroline looked more bored than scared. How could Maddie have faced Cameron if...? She stopped herself. She wouldn't think about it. She couldn't.

"Yes, we can go."

The rain had let up some, the worst of the storm having blown over while they had waited for the authorities to arrive. She watched the deputy turn off the flashing lights on his cruiser and drive away. The man whose car had struck Maddie's had already gone. She turned the key in the ignition, levered the gearshift to drive and said a simple prayer before depressing the accelerator and easing back onto the road. The mile to Mockingbird Lane was the longest mile Maddie had ever driven.

It was with wilting relief that she turned up Cameron's drive. The porch light was on. It burned brightly through the hazy darkness of the storm and approaching twilight.

"We're home!" Caroline cried from the back seat, already fumbling with her safety restraint. Cam had stepped out of the house and stood on the porch, hip cocked, a lazy smile crooking up the corners of his mouth. For one long, yearning moment Maddie wished this truly were her home, her family.

"It took you long enough," he called as they hurried up the walk through the rain.

"We had a little problem," Maddie hedged. "I hope dinner is salvageable."

She needed a moment. She wanted to stop shaking

before telling Cameron how he'd entrusted her to bring home his daughter safely and she'd nearly gotten her killed.

But Caroline supplied cheerfully, "We got into a wreck. But don't worry, Daddy, the policeman said the car is drivable."

Maddie braced herself for his censure. Surely he would chew her out for her recklessness. In her mind, she could hear the echo of Ted's diatribe as she lay in the hospital after the other accident. He'd used ugly language, called her even uglier names. She was sure that grief over Michael's death had prompted him to say the words, but that didn't make them any less true, or Maddie any less deserving of his loathing.

"Are you all right?" The last thing she'd expected was concern, but it was there in the cadence of Cam's voice and the soft comfort of his touch as he ran his hands up and down her arms. "You're shaking. Let's get you inside."

She was pale as death and trembling like a leaf. His daughter appeared fine and apparently Maddie's car had survived in okay shape, but Maddie was another story. Cam had taken one look at her bleached complexion and known she was on the verge of splintering apart. He hustled her inside, steering her to the couch, where she sank down less than gracefully when her knees buckled and her bravado gave way.

"Sprite, why don't you go get Maddie a glass of water?"

As he would a child, Cam helped Maddie out of her jacket and then brushed the damp hair back from her face.

"I'm a mess," she murmured.

He knew she wasn't referring to her appearance from the way her eyes filled with tears. Vanity might make some women cry, but not Maddie. He sat down next to her, looped an arm over her shoulder.

Pulling her close, he whispered, "You're not a mess. Car accidents leave most people a little unsettled, and you've got a better reason than most to be upset since you were in a bad one before."

Caroline returned with the water, which Maddie took and dutifully sipped.

"Did she tell you that some guy runned us off the road?" his daughter asked.

Cam's heart squeezed so painfully he didn't even think to correct her grammar. He made his tone even and tried to keep his expression neutral when he said, "Is that so?"

"Yeah, he runned us and the guy behind us off the road. Maddie swerved just in time, but the guy behind us couldn't stop and then there was this loud noise and the car jumped and everything when he hit us. Good thing Maddie has bumpers on her car," Caroline finished sagely.

"Good thing," Cam repeated, and he thanked his lucky stars that God hadn't seen fit to pluck another important person—or persons—from his life.

"I'm starving, Daddy. When are we going to eat?"

Cam had lost his appetite and Maddie looked as if keeping down food would be next to impossible, but he made his tone upbeat when he replied, "Soup's on. Hope you like your chili hot and your grilled cheese gooey."

Somehow, Maddie made it through the meal sitting in Cameron's homey kitchen. She smiled and listened to Caroline's outrageous chatter. She managed to spoon down half a bowl of spicy chili. She even nibbled on a wedge of cheesy sandwich. But she kept thinking about the accident and what could have happened had she not swerved in time. She didn't need to use her imagination, memory served her well enough.

She glanced at the cat-shaped clock that hung over the window by the sink. It was well past seven o'clock now, and growing darker outside by the minute. She dreaded the thought of driving home on wet pavement.

"Are you done?" Cameron asked, nodding toward her bowl.

"Yes." She managed a smile. "I can't eat another bite. It was very good, Cameron."

"Old family recipe. Hormel family, that is," he added, sending her a wink. He stood, carried both of their bowls to the sink and rinsed them off. After drying his hands on the dish towel, he turned and leaned casually against the counter.

"You know, Maddie, I was thinking. You could stay with me tonight." His face colored after he said it. "I mean, you could sleep in my bed." After that interesting offer, his face grew even redder. "What I mean is, I'll take the couch."

Caroline wiggled in her seat and clapped her hands together excitedly, oblivious to her father's discomfort.

"Yippee! A sleepover party. Daddy, can I stay up late with you and Maddie?"

Cameron's gaze shifted to Maddie for one long, measuring moment that had her forgetting all about the afternoon's near tragedy. She swore her skin felt singed when he said, "We'll see, sprite. We'll see."

Chapter Eight

Maddie stayed.

Cam hadn't been sure she would when he made the offer during dinner, even though she had looked pale and tired and much too shaky to drive. He supposed he could have taken her home. That, of course, would have been the polite thing to do. But Cam had liked just a little too much the thought of Maddie being in his bed when he woke in the morning, even if he would be on the couch.

His hands stilled on the sheet he was stretching over the cushions, and his gaze fixed on the gold band he'd taken off before each date, but always—always—put back on. He would never stop loving his wife, he knew. Nothing and no one could change that, or dim the memories of their happy years.

And yet…

He eased himself down onto the couch, his emotions reeling as realization dawned. As much as he loved Angie and the life they'd shared, he was moving on. It had been happening for quite some time, in tiny baby steps rather than giant leaps.

He'd been slowly falling in love. With Maddie Daniels.

The magnitude of this personal epiphany left him staggered, but Caroline didn't seem to notice when she skipped into the room a moment later, holding a dog-eared copy of *Cinderella*.

"Daddy, can you read me and Maddie a bedtime story?" she asked as she plopped the book in his lap.

"Maddie and me," he corrected. Cam craved a stiff drink and a few hours alone to sort out these new emotions, which seemed to be as hopelessly tangled as a string of Christmas lights, but he forced a smile for his daughter's benefit. "Just give me a minute to finish making up the couch, okay?"

Caroline dashed down the hallway, her small feet barely skimming the floorboards in her excitement, as Cam lowered his head into his hands. He needed days, but he had mere minutes to find his equilibrium.

I'm falling in love again. And Cam thought he understood why they called it "falling." The prospect left him a bit scraped up and raw, even as he also felt surprised and…excited. Some of it could be pegged on hormones. That would be easy since he understood attraction, and he could admit he had responded physically to Maddie from that first meeting several months earlier. But far more than fragile beauty and slender curves had sneaked past his defenses and burrowed into his heart. It was the whole improbable package of earnest friend, caring confidante and shy, self-conscious siren.

Cam found that he wanted to see Maddie smile more often. More than that, he wanted to be the one responsible for those smiles. And, he wanted to know why happiness seemed to come so hard for her. Somehow he thought it went deeper than a serious auto accident and a wrecked marriage.

Now, however, was not the time for probing, either his emotions or her explanations. So he curbed his curiosity and finished spreading out the blankets, noting with a sigh of resignation that the living room couch was a good foot shorter than he was.

Caroline's room was dark and quiet when he stopped at the threshold, ready to read her the promised bedtime story. He had a good idea where he could find her, though. Across the hall, the door to his bedroom was ajar and high-pitched giggles spilled out from the crack. He couldn't help but smile in return. There was something infectious about a child's laughter. He knocked once before pushing open the door and stepping inside. Then he stopped, sobered and felt his heart squeeze at the sight that greeted him. Maddie and Caroline were seated cross-legged atop the comforter and Maddie was painting his daughter's tiny, well-bitten fingernails a festive hot pink.

He liked seeing his daughter enjoying a moment of feminine foolishness, a little female bonding that fate had cruelly denied her with her own mother. Oh, he tried to paint Caroline's nails now and again, but he found his hands too big and bulky and hers too small and fidgety to do justice to such a precise task. Eve was better at it, but she was understandably too busy with her boys to do it as often as Caroline would have liked. Maddie, however, seemed to be enjoying herself as much as his daughter was. She'd be a natural as a parent, he thought.

"If I come in, do I have to paint my nails?"

"Oh, Daddy!" Caroline rolled her eyes. "Boys don't wear nail polish. Do they, Maddie?"

Maddie was too busy tugging the ends of the T-shirt he'd loaned her over her exposed knees to do more than shake her head. She'd acted quickly, but not before Cam saw the web of scars that covered one leg. She appeared embarrassed, as if she expected him to be repulsed. Repulsion, however, was a far cry from what Cam was feeling as his hungry gaze took in Maddie, wearing his maize-and-blue Michigan shirt, sitting in the center of his big bed like a present to be unwrapped at Christmas. He swallowed hard, fought the wild urge to tell Caroline to go to her room, and then bolt the door once she'd scampered out. Some anemic remnant of chivalry had him reaching into the closet and handing Maddie his robe.

"I promised Caroline a bedtime story." He motioned with the book toward the door. "Come on, kiddo. Tell Maddie good-night."

"No, Daddy, read it in here. Please. You can read it to both of us." Caroline scooted over on the bed, pulling back the comforter and diving beneath its downy warmth. Then she patted the empty place beside her. "Come on, Daddy, get in."

"Watch those wet nails, sprite," he admonished. Over his daughter's head, he glanced uncertainly at

Maddie, who had shrugged into the robe, but stayed on top of the comforter.

She nodded once, and then said softly, "Yes, Cameron, read to both of us."

Cam sank down on the mattress, his gaze still locked with Maddie's. Like her, he decided to stay on top of the covers. Why, he couldn't have said. It wasn't as if something sweaty and sinful could happen while they were wearing clothes, a child wedged snuggly between them. Yet this seemed the safest bet.

He propped his head on a pillow and began reading. Caroline knew the story by heart and so she recited it along with him, mimicking the voices of the fairy godmother as well as those of Cinderella's devious stepsisters. When they came to the part where Prince Charming slides the glass slipper onto Cinderella's foot, Cam reached under the covers to tweak his daughter's toes. It was an old game. He always tickled her first, and then kissed her instep. Tonight, however, she wriggled free of his grasp.

"No, no, Daddy, not me. Do Maddie this time. This can be her turn." She grinned engagingly, and he couldn't help thinking his daughter had picked one heck of a time to practice her sharing skills. Ah, well, as a father, what could he do but oblige her?

Maddie's eyes went wide and her breath hitched when she figured out his intent.

"Cameron, no."

Even issued in that formal way of hers, it didn't sound much like a protest. He decided to ignore it as he leaned over and fished out one of the feet she had tucked beneath the folds of the robe. It was slender, fine-boned, battered…perfect. He traced a fingertip over a scar that ran from her big toe to her ankle, stopping only because Caroline was watching and because he knew he wouldn't have the willpower to end his exploration if he took it much further.

"Kiss it, Daddy," Caroline coached, clapping her hands together and giggling. She turned to Maddie, grinned. "It's part of our game. He has to kiss your foot."

Just a game, Maddie told herself, it was just a game. Still, the air seemed to back up in her lungs as she watched Cameron. His hands were warm and roughened from work, and she thought she understood what heaven would be like when they skimmed her instep and stroked her ankle. A simple touch, and yet more sensuous than the most brazen caresses she'd ever experienced as a married woman. Cameron's gaze was intense and it never left hers as he bent to kiss her sensitive arch. She sucked in a breath, held it, and was dimly aware that her fingers had fisted in the folds of the comforter.

"Are you ticklish?"

It took Maddie a moment to realize that Caroline was speaking to her.

"Wh-what?" She unclenched her fists, tried to relax.

"Are you ticklish?" The little girl's brow puckered thoughtfully. "I guess not. When Daddy kisses my foot I always start laughing."

"She does look quite serious, doesn't she, sprite."

For all his teasing words, he looked quite serious himself, and he sounded winded. Ridiculous, Maddie told herself. Surely she had only imagined that Cameron was feeling as wound up as she was. Then he leaned over his daughter to brush his fingertips down the slope of Maddie's cheek. The gesture was friendly, hardly intimate given their wide-eyed audience of one, but his hand—that big, callused, competent hand—was shaking.

Cam had tried to sleep after bidding Maddie goodnight and tucking Caroline beneath her pink Barbie bedspread. But he'd lain awake for a couple of hours on his makeshift bed before giving in to his insomnia and getting back up. Now he sat in the dark on the front porch, drinking a beer, a cold, wet wind slapping his face. It made his eyes water, his cheeks sting. It chewed through the tattered sweatshirt he wore, but it didn't do anything to cool the heat burning inside him. He had a lot of thinking to do, and he did his best thinking outdoors. And so he sat on the porch and sipped his beer, surrounded by the scents of frosted earth and dying leaves.

Angie had loved the fall. She'd called it God's color palate and had honored the season by wearing vivid yellows and rusty oranges, and covering the kitchen table in a festive leaf-print cloth. Every October she insisted she and Cam go on at least one hayride and take a tour of a nearby orchard and cider mill, even though their farm had several dozen apple trees on the south side of the cherry orchard. But Angie had had a weakness for apple-cinnamon donuts and fresh cider. And Cam had had a weakness for Angie.

He thought about the woman sleeping in his bed. She was so different from his late wife, who had grabbed hold of life with both hands and lived it fully, even when death had circled close and cast its long shadow over their lives. Maddie, by contrast, was serious, uncertain, reserved. But Maddie shared one fundamental attribute with Cam's late wife: she had a kind, caring heart. Maybe that's what had drawn him to her even when he'd tried to push her—and thoughts of her—away.

Cam's beer was empty and the cold had begun to make him shiver. He walked into the house, his footsteps sure in the familiar surroundings, despite the darkness. At the couch, he toed off his sneakers and stripped off his sweatshirt and jeans before climbing beneath the covers. His feet poked over one armrest, and his back already felt tight and kinked. He debated going in to snuggle up with Caroline. Her single bed sported a pink canopy, but he didn't consider it a threat to his masculinity if it meant getting a couple of hours of sleep before dawn broke and the day began.

He was just swinging his legs over the side of the couch when he heard the scream.

Maddie hadn't woke up sweating and shaking from the nightmare in months, but she jolted from a sound sleep now, a scream ripe on her lips, her heart racing and body bracing for the collision to come. When it didn't, she sat up in bed, letting the damp covers pool around her and hugged her good knee to her chest. In the moonlight, it took her a moment to get her bearings. The sleekly curved cherry footboard told her she was in Cameron's bed with the silence of the countryside yawning around her. A quick glance at the illuminated face of the alarm clock beside the bed told her it was just past four.

As she was trying to decide whether to get up and splash some cold water on her face or pull the comforter over her head and wait for morning, a slight rapping sounded at the door. She reached for Cam's robe, which lay over the foot of the bed, then stood and pulled it on before turning on the bedside lamp and opening the door a crack. Cameron stood in the hallway, hair mussed, his face slightly darkened with the shadow of a beard. He was shirtless and wore a pair of jeans that appeared to have been pulled on hastily—the fly was not quite buttoned.

"I heard you scream," he said, concern etched into the planes of his face.

She felt her face flush. "Did I scream?"

"Not really loud. You didn't wake Caroline. It sounded muffled. I..." He shifted from foot to foot. "I probably only heard it because I couldn't sleep."

"That couch can't be very comfortable," she sympathized.

"Not especially, no."

"It was really kind of you not only to let me stay, but to give up your bed for me."

"I wanted you there." He glanced past her into the room, his gaze settling on the rumpled sheets before it returned to her. When he spoke again, his voice was a seductive whisper. "I wanted you in my bed.

To tell you the truth, Maddie, I wanted to be in there with you.''

She sucked in a breath, shook her head, seeking to clear it.

''I want you, Maddie. I know I told you once before that I didn't, but I was lying. To you, but mostly to myself. I want you.''

Hope soared high just before it crashed and burned on the barren landscape of her life. Maddie shook her head again, this time in denial.

''Why does that surprise you?''

She found her voice, even though it sounded too breathy and uncertain to belong to her. ''I'm flattered, really. But I'm not...'' She fluttered a hand, unable to finish.

''Not what? Not beautiful? My God, Maddie, would you look in a mirror? Or pay attention next time you walk past a park bench full of guys. A cane in your hand and a few scars don't stop them from looking or from wanting. They didn't stop me.''

He came into the room, forcing her to retreat until the backs of her legs pressed against the bed. She sank to the mattress, too shocked to stand. Cameron leaned forward, gently cradled her face between his rough palms. Even if he hadn't kissed her, covering her mouth so expertly with his own, the hunger smoldering in his eyes would have rendered her speechless. Need and feelings spiraled inside her, twining together, growing stronger as he turned her, brought her legs to the mattress and then pressed her back onto the pillow. He followed her down with his own body, taking most of his weight on his elbows. Still, she liked the feel of him on top of her, solid and broad and warm. She liked even more the intimate way their bodies fitted together, soft curves molding to hard muscles as if scored one to the other. She allowed her hands to explore, sliding them up his bare back. His flesh quivered beneath her touch and she felt him suck in a breath as he nipped her earlobe.

"Let me make love to you, Maddie." His voice was a hoarse whisper when he added, "I've wanted to for some time now."

Saying yes would have been easy. Never before had she been swept up in a passion so overwhelming that it nearly overruled reason. But this did. It briefly eclipsed sanity, defied the tidy explanation of hormones or chemical reactions. Ultimately, however, it didn't, couldn't overrule her conscience. Cameron didn't know what he was saying. He didn't know what she had done.

The hands she had laid against his chest in desire a moment earlier now pushed against his shoulders in desperation. She had to get away before she did something foolish, something unforgivable, like letting him believe they could share a future as anything more than friends. When he shifted off of her, she rolled away from him and sat up on the mattress, feeling instantly chilled.

"I can't." She combed shaking fingers through her tangled hair and dared to look at him over her shoulder. In the lamplight, he appeared to be as unsettled as she was.

"Why?"

A simple question to which there was no simple answer.

"I have my reasons."

He swung his long, well-muscled legs over the side of the bed and sat next to her, blowing out a long, frustrated breath.

"I'd like to hear them." There was a spark of belligerence in his tone.

"Can it just be enough to know that if circumstances were different...if I were different..." Her voice trailed away. "I'm sorry, Cameron, but I can't."

Cam stilled one of her fidgety hands by taking it in his own, and then tugged on it until Maddie looked at him. He wanted to understand, but he couldn't. She was as drawn to him as he was to her, he'd stake his life on it, and yet she held back. Maybe she needed the actual words for what he was feeling. Maybe, he thought wryly, he needed to say them—aloud—so that she knew the only people sharing this bed were the two of them.

"You know, I sat on the front porch for a long time tonight trying to figure out what I'm going to do about you."

"Do about me?"

"Yeah. I loved Angie. I figured she'd be the only woman I could ever feel all tied up over." He looked down at his hand as he said it, and at the wedding band that was still nestled there. Slowly, he slipped it off and clenched it in his palm briefly before setting it on the nightstand. He heard Maddie suck in a quick breath. Looking at her, he continued, "But, you know what? I was wrong. As much as I swore I wouldn't, and as hard as I tried not to, I'm falling in love again. With you.''

He smiled after he said it. The words didn't betray his first love, he realized. They complimented it. In an odd way, they honored his late wife, proving that because he had been loved so well once, he was capable of loving again.

While he felt relieved, cleansed, Maddie appeared horrified. She stood, stumbled away from him.

''No, Cameron. Don't love me.''

He stood as well and reached for her, but she backed away, shaking her head.

''Why? Why shouldn't I love you?'' In his frustration, his voice rose to a near shout. With an effort he lowered it, but he was sure his blood pressure remained elevated. He could feel the pulse pounding in his temples. He'd just bared his soul, surrendered his heart, and she was essentially telling him no thanks.

''You deserve someone better than me, Cameron.''

Of all the responses he'd expected, that one floored him. Someone better than Maddie Daniels? But he thought he understood the reason behind her words.

''I don't care about the scars. They make you who you are—the woman I've fallen in love with.'' Repeating the words gave them strength, and in turn they gave him courage. He pulled her into his arms, nuzzling her neck despite her rigid posture, dropping a kiss onto the tiny mole that had intrigued him from the start. ''I didn't think I'd ever feel this way again.''

She ripped herself away from his embrace, wrapping her hands around her middle as if in physical pain. Tears leaked from her eyes and streaked unchecked down her pale cheeks. If she had looked horrified a moment earlier, she looked mortified and utterly miserable now.

"It's not the scars, Cameron. It's…it's what they represent." Her voice was a hoarse whisper when she added, "You don't know what I've done."

"Done?"

"Ted…" She choked off a sob. "He left me."

Relief surged through Cam. "So you're divorced. I don't care. I know I said I wouldn't be interested in someone whose marriage had failed, but I met your ex-husband. Remember? Even from that brief encounter, I understood that the guy was heartless and a fool besides. If he left, it wasn't your fault, at least not entirely. He wasn't good enough for *you,* Maddie."

"He had no choice."

"We all have choices. His choice was to leave you when you were recovering from a serious injury. You needed him and he walked. That makes him a first-class jerk in my book." An unpleasant thought knifed through him then. He forced himself to ask, "Do you still love him?"

She shook her head and Cam felt the muscles in his stomach relax.

"I don't know that I ever loved him the way that I love…" She stopped herself, closed her eyes. "Don't love me, Cameron," she pleaded again.

Cam felt his patience wane. He was sure she had been about to admit she loved him, too. In frustration, he snapped, "You disappoint me, Maddie. What happened to all your sermons about true love and finding someone special to spend time with? Was that all just a bunch of talk?''

''No. I believe it. It just won't happen for me.''

He raked a hand through his hair. ''Whatever sin it is that you feel you must atone for, it must be a real doozy.''

''It is.'' She walked to the bathroom, her gait slower and more stilted than ever before. She hovered in the doorway for a moment before turning, her expression so sad he forgot his anger.

''I killed my son.''

Chapter Nine

I killed my son.

Maddie's words seemed to echo in the quiet room. *What did she mean, she had killed her son? What son?* Cam took a step toward the closed bathroom door. He wanted answers, needed them. Desperately. Only the sound of her weeping prevented him from pounding on the door and demanding an explanation. He swore softly. Now was not the time.

"Daddy, why is Maddie crying?"

Cam turned to find his daughter in the doorway, rubbing the sleep out of a pair of eyes that were wide and troubled. From experience, Cam knew that children didn't like it when the adults in their life appeared sad or scared. So, he sat on the edge of the bed and held out a hand. Caroline scampered to him and hopped onto the mattress. She wrapped her small arms around him and clung like a burr while he thought about the best way to explain.

He settled on "Maddie had a bad dream, sprite. It woke her up and made her sad."

"It sounded like you were arguing," she pointed out.

Small people had really big ears, he thought with a sigh, grateful she hadn't understood the text of their argument or come bursting in a moment earlier when he'd been lying atop Maddie, hormones running so hot and thick he'd forgotten he had a young, impressionable daughter sleeping just down the hallway.

"We weren't really arguing. We were just…"

"Discusting?"

"Discussing," he corrected her. "Yeah, we were just discussing some things."

"Then why was she crying?"

"I told you, she had a bad dream."

"When I have bad dreams, you always make me hot cocoa. Do you think that might help Maddie?"

Maddie's troubles went well beyond anything that could be fixed with a mug full of steaming calories and sugarcoated caffeine, but he was no match for his daughter's earnest face.

"I think she might like that." He planted a noisy kiss on Caroline's forehead and snatched her up into his arms. With one last glance in the direction of the bathroom, he said, "Come on, sprite. Let's go make that cocoa."

The water in the kettle had just started to boil, but over the shrill whistle, Cam heard the front door snap shut. A moment later a car's engine fired to life. He didn't need to walk to the living room and look out the big window to know Maddie was leaving. But he

did so, anyway. He watched the headlights of her automobile as it lurched backward down his long, winding drive. Then she turned it onto the dirt road,
gunned the engine and was gone. Part of his heart left
with her. Cam rubbed his chest, felt a raw ache there
that he hadn't thought he'd ever experience again. He
wasn't sure whether he wanted to curse Maddie Daniels or rail at fate.

He made hot cocoa instead.

Maddie stumbled into her small apartment just as
dawn began to dapple the sky a glorious, glowing
orange. The morning's beauty seemed to mock her
despair. She wasn't sure how she had gotten home,
only that in her desperation to flee from Cameron, she
had not cared about her personal safety. She didn't
bother to pull off her jacket or remove her shoes. She
made it only as far as the couch, where she collapsed.
The sobs that shuddered from her left her throat as
raw and aching as her heart. She cried for the child
who would never be, she cried for the woman she
was and she cried for the man who said he loved her,
but who surely must despise her now.

Late in the afternoon, Cam's doorbell rang. He
bolted from the couch, where he'd been reclining and
watching the football game. Brooding, actually, since
it occurred to him that he didn't know whether the
Lions or Green Bay Packers were up at the moment.

She'd come back, was all he could think as he hurried to the door. Maddie had returned. But when he
flung open the heavy oak door, his smile warm and

his questions held in check, it was his sister-in-law
who stood on the front porch.

"Are you going to invite me in?" Eve asked with
a laugh that had cold air wreathing misty white
around her face. The temperature seemed to have
dropped another ten degrees since the day before,
leaving the mercury to hover around forty.

"Of course." Cam stepped back, feeling foolish.

Eve hustled inside, unzipping a puffy down jacket.
"It's frigid out there," she commented, rubbing her
hands together briskly. "And it's not even Thanksgiving yet. I swear winter arrives earlier every year."

Cam forced himself to laugh and, falling back on
small talk, quipped, "It's not officially winter. And
you *say* that every year."

"Well, that doesn't make it any less true."

"Aunt Eve!" A small, dark-haired tornado swept
into the room and snagged Eve around her waist.
"Where are Trevor and Tucker?"

"They went with their father to the sporting goods
store. There's nothing I want in hunter's orange, so I
declined. Anyway, I thought I'd pop in, see how my
favorite niece is doing." She smoothed back Caroline's hair, and Cam realized with a start that it hadn't
been combed yet that day. Indeed, if the child hadn't
dressed herself, she would still be wearing her pajamas, hot cocoa stain down the front and all. Cam still
wore the jeans and sweatshirt from the night before.

"So what are you two doing today?" Eve asked.

"Being lazy." Cam shrugged.

His daughter grinned guilelessly and apropos of

nothing announced, "Maddie spent the night last night."

Cam groaned. No secret was safe with a child—not that Maddie's staying the night had been a secret or something Cam was ashamed of. He just knew how it would look, how Eve would see it, so he had planned to keep it to himself.

"Really?" Sure enough, there was a smile in Eve's eyes, and a healthy amount of speculation, when she turned her gaze to Cam. Her dark brows shot up. "The whole night?"

"It's not what you think." Even to his own ears the words sounded defensive, guilty. He fought the urge to fidget under his sister-in-law's inquiring stare, dipping his hands into the pockets of his jeans and shifting his weight to his other leg.

"But do you want it to be what I think?" she asked softly, seriously.

Cam glanced at his daughter, blew out a breath.

"Go play with your Barbies, sprite. Aunt Eve and I have some things to talk about."

"Grown-ups," she muttered with a roll of her eyes. "Can I have an ice-cream sundae for dinner?"

Cam ruffled her hair. "Dessert," he compromised, well aware he'd been had.

Eve waited until she heard the click of her niece's bedroom door. "Well?"

He shoved his hands back into his pockets and paced to the front window, where he looked out briefly before turning back to face her. "Yeah, I want it to be what you think."

Eve went to him, laid a reassuring hand on his

shoulder. "There's no reason to feel guilty, Cam. You're a grown man. You've been alone for three years. It's natural to feel…well, you know, that way about an attractive woman."

He took her hand, squeezed it. "Eve, it's…it's not just about sex."

She stepped back, myriad emotions playing on her lovely face—surprise, elation, then resigned sadness, the source of which he thought he understood.

"My God, you love her." She clapped a hand over her mouth after saying it, as if wishing she could shove the words back inside.

Eve had made it clear that she wanted him to date again, to find someone else and move on with his life, but saying it and being confronted with the reality of it were two different things. Cam knew that despite all Eve's well-intentioned words, his falling in love with another woman had to hurt. It had to make Angie's death all the more final, her life all the more past tense.

"That was my reaction at first, too. But I love Maddie."

He dragged a hand through his uncombed hair. God only knew how he must look. Probably like some lovesick teenager who'd been dumped right before the prom.

Eve's voice was cautious but also curious when she asked, "Does she love you back?"

Cam thought about the woman who had dropped a bombshell on him early that morning and then run from his home, so eager to be gone that she'd braved dark, wet roads.

"I don't know. She's…it's complicated."

"Oh, Cam." Eve sighed. "Love is always complicated at first." She gave him a sisterly hug. "I'm happy for you. Really. I am happy for you."

"I'm glad. I wish I could be happy for me right now, too."

"It will work out. I know it will. I've seen the way Maddie looks at you. I told Richard after that first meeting that she was losing her heart to you. Whatever obstacle seems so insurmountable right now, the two of you will work it out. She'll come around."

He nodded once, hoping his sister-in-law was right. "I can wait," he replied, more for his own benefit than for Eve's.

Waiting, however, proved to be a true test of endurance. Cam had been patient. Despite his gut-gnawing curiosity, he had held off for a couple of days before trying to contact Maddie, hoping to give her some time to compose herself. He had no wish to carelessly probe an obviously still-throbbing wound. For his thoughtfulness, he'd gotten nowhere. Weeks had passed, and Maddie was still adroitly dodging his telephone calls, an easy feat since he didn't have her home phone number and had to contact her at work. After hours, no one answered, even though he'd bet his last dollar she was there. During the day, her receptionist, Lisa, had gotten quite adept at making excuses for her boss's inaccessibility, but Cam knew that's just what they were—excuses.

But even Cam's considerable patience had a limit. And he'd long since reached it. He pulled his truck to a stop in the municipal parking lot, noting with a grunt of frustration that Maddie's silver Volvo was not there. He'd wait, he decided, all day, if it came to that.

The receptionist sighed when he entered, and stopped cracking her gum long enough to say, "Miss Daniels is, like, real busy, Mr. Foley. She won't be able to see you today."

His mood brightened fractionally. "She's in?"

"Yeah, and busy," the young woman stressed again. Her words gave away her youth, but her tone took on that of a kindergarten teacher instructing a recalcitrant five-year-old when she added, "Maybe you could, like, call ahead next time. You know, make an appointment."

"Why, so she can conveniently be gone when I come in? Uh-uh." Cam shook his head and crossed his arms belligerently over his chest. "Tell her I'm here."

"Mr. Foley, she won't see you." Lisa sounded almost sorry about it. Or sorry for him. Cam wasn't sure he liked that change in attitude. He'd rather she be full of pith than give him that pitying, doe-eyed stare. He'd been getting enough of that from Eve for the past few weeks.

He thought about barging into Maddie's office again, but he did have some pride.

"I'll wait."

He picked up a magazine and slouched into one of the armless chairs near the front window.

"Look, Mr. Foley, you seem like a reasonable guy—"

He held up a hand to silence her. "Don't mistake me for reasonable. I stopped being reasonable about thirteen unreturned phone calls ago." He sent her a thin smile and enunciated as clearly as possible, "I. Will. Wait."

She rolled her eyes, her meager reserve of pity apparently used up. It was almost a relief when she shrugged and in a bored voice replied, "Whatever."

She disappeared into her boss's office, presumably to announce his arrival. *Now we're getting somewhere,* Cam thought, smugly satisfied. Four cups of bad coffee and seven magazines later, he revised his opinion.

Maddie left him cooling his heels for more than an hour after the receptionist clocked out for the day. The wait did nothing to improve his mood. When she finally stepped out of her office, leather briefcase in one hand, wool coat thrown carelessly over her other arm, he was irritable and hungry and nursing a caffeine headache that had the two lobes of his brain acting as cymbals.

She set her case on the reception desk and pulled on her coat. As she worked the large black buttons through the holes, she said, "Cameron, I'm terribly sorry I kept you waiting, but I'm afraid it's been an impossibly busy day, and it's not over yet. Tomorrow should be better. Perhaps we could meet downtown somewhere for lunch. My treat."

She offered her polite apology and gracious suggestion without bothering to look at him. That and the slight tremor in her hands revealed her unease.

"Not lunch tomorrow, Maddie. We need to talk."

When she would have walked past him, he gripped her arm, forcing her to face him. "Now."

Nerves fluttered in her stomach like the beating of a thousand tiny birds' wings. Maddie tried to soothe them by retreating behind brisk formality.

"Very well, Cameron. I suppose I can reschedule my plans for the evening." Plans, she thought in bemusement, that had included a nice soak in her bathtub and fertilizing her plants before tuning in for Jay Leno's monologue.

"Good."

He steered her out of the building, gripping her elbow, she swore, not in support or to prevent her from slipping on the icy walk, but as if he expected her to try to flee.

"Is your car in the shop?" he asked as he opened the door to his truck and helped her inside.

"My car?" It occurred to her then that he didn't know she lived mere blocks away and walked to work. She smoothed the long coat over her knees and evaded, "Oh, I found another way to the office today."

They drove in a silence as cold and stinging as the wind whipping off the bay. When she didn't think she could take a moment more of it, he surprised her by pulling the car to a stop outside a restaurant that specialized in soothing piano music and hearty steak dinners.

At her questioning gaze, he said, "I'm starving. We'll eat first. I talk better on a full stomach."

Why, Maddie wondered, did it feel as if this would be her Last Supper?

Cameron may have been vibrating with irritation and impatience, but Maddie couldn't fault his manners. He opened her door and ushered her inside the restaurant, where he pulled out her chair once they'd been shown to an intimate table in the rear of the crowded establishment.

"I'll have a beer. Whatever's on tap is fine," he told the pretty young waitress who had come for their beverage orders.

Maddie wanted a drink, too. Something strong enough to chisel away at her nerves, but she didn't dare drop her guard. If she did, she might cry. Or worse—much worse—beg for his understanding.

"Ice water, please." Maddie cleared her throat, all too aware that after her confession about her son, Cameron already must think that ice water coursed through her veins.

When the waitress had retreated, Maddie folded her hands primly before her on the table and braced herself for Cameron's questions, his accusations.

"I've missed you." The quiet admission caused her heart to squeeze.

"I've missed…" She looked away from the tenderness in his eyes, the love that—unbelievably—remained there. It was a love she had no right to.

"I'm sure you must have questions after…after what was said the last time we saw each other."

Cam had questions, all right. Dozens of them, hundreds of them. They'd been humming around in his head for weeks, eating at his concentration, chasing away sleep. Confronted with her quiet misery, however, he could not bring himself to interrogate her.

"I can wait until you can tell me without my asking."

She smiled, her tone a little watery when she replied, "I would have sworn the man who confronted me in my office twenty minutes ago had run out of patience."

He reached across the table, stroked his fingers over the back of her hand. He spoke the truth when he replied, "I just needed to see you."

"Oh, Cameron." The misery was back. He saw it before she squeezed her eyes shut, snatched her hand away. "How can you even look at me after what I did? My son died. It was my fault."

Died. That was a felony charge away from *killed.* Cam hadn't thought Maddie capable of murder, but it still was a relief to hear her say it, and, since the opening was there, he took it. "I want to understand, Maddie. I'll listen if you want to talk about it."

When she finally began speaking, her voice was soft, filled with a sadness almost more mesmerizing than her chilling words.

"I was driving back to the summerhouse Ted and I had on Old Mission peninsula. I'd gone shopping to buy things for the nursery. I was so excited about the baby and I had seen some lovely things at a store in town earlier in the day. I insisted on going, even though Ted told me not to, or at least to wait until he got back from an afternoon meeting with a developer about some lakefront property we owned near Suttons Bay. But I went, anyway. It was raining when I left the shop. I decided to stop for a bite to eat, wait out the storm. But the weather just seemed to get worse and it was growing late. The roads were wet and slick when I left the restaurant.''

She squeezed her eyes shut, took a fortifying breath.

''Don't, Maddie,'' Cam begged. He didn't need to hear her tell him what happened next. Her anguished expression revealed it quite plainly. But she shook her head, opening eyes that were bright with unshed tears, and continued.

''I saw the headlights coming straight at me, just like—''

''Just like that night when you were bringing Caroline home.''

She gave a jerky nod. ''I didn't react quickly enough, though. I felt paralyzed. It was a truck, a semi, hauling a load of logs. The cab clipped the front of the car on my side, spun it around so that the back end slammed into the trailer. The car flipped end over end then, down a hill, and landed on its side in a water-filled ditch, or so the police told me later. I don't remember much, except for screaming and the blinding pain I felt when the steering wheel crushed into my abdomen. My baby didn't have a chance,'' she finished on a sob.

Her hands clutched her stomach and the last puzzle piece fell into place. Her son had died before birth, and misguided though it was, Maddie had assigned the blame to herself.

''It was an accident. You weren't responsible.''

''I was,'' she replied with such quiet conviction that he knew trying to persuade her otherwise would take more than a few well-chosen words in a public restaurant.

The waitress had just brought their beverages and taken their orders when a woman of about thirty called out, "Maddie, is that you?"

As the woman walked to their table, Cam watched in admiration as Maddie dredged up a smile.

"Melinda, hello. I haven't seen you in ages. Are you and Steve up for the skiing? I hear the base at Crystal Mountain is already excellent."

"Steve skis, I shop," Melinda corrected her with an annoyingly high-pitched laugh.

Cam took in the Rock of Gibraltar diamond on her left hand and the gold that dripped from her earlobes, and decided the sable-wrapped Melinda was probably very good at her avocation.

"Steve's out warming up the car, but I had to stop over and see if it really was Maddie Stewart who walked in while we were finishing our coffee."

"I go by Daniels now," Maddie explained. "I took back my maiden name after the divorce."

"Ah, yes. Nasty business, that," Melinda commiserated. "But it looks like you've both landed on your feet." She shot an assessing glance in Cam's direction. He smiled politely, not the least bit fooled. She was dying to know every last detail of their relationship so she could pass it on to friends.

"Forgive me for being so rude, Melinda. This is Cameron Foley." To Cam she said, "Melinda and her husband have a place just up the beach from the summerhouse Ted owns. They're also from Grosse Pointe."

"Hello."

"Nice to meet you, Cameron." She directed her attention back to Maddie. "Speaking of Ted, you heard of course that he remarried."

"Yes." Maddie said, nodding. "In fact, I believe you're the one who told me that."

Cam heard the subtle reprimand in Maddie's tone, but, gossip that Melinda was, she remained oblivious. "That's right. I did. Awfully quick on the heels of your divorce, if you know what I mean."

Cam knew what she meant. He'd questioned Ted's fidelity himself, but he'd had too much respect for Maddie's feelings to do so aloud. Melinda showed no such compassion.

"Did you know that his new wife just had a baby?"

Maddie smiled, but Cam knew what it cost her. "No. I knew they were expecting. How nice for them."

"Yes, they had a boy," Melinda said, clearly relishing her role as the bearer of painful news.

"A boy," Maddie echoed, the smile slipping slightly. "Ted really wanted a boy."

"Yes. The Stewart family name is apparently assured for another generation. You know how pathetically old-fashioned they are when it comes to heirs and assuring the lineage," Melinda drawled. "Ted seemed very pleased when I ran into him at the club shortly after the birth. He was passing out cigars, chest all puffed up. All he could talk about was his little Michael."

Maddie gasped, and even her proper manners deserted her, allowing the naked pain she felt to show on her face. "But our son was Michael."

"Oh, my. I didn't know. I'm sorry." Melinda pursed her lips smpathetically. The feral gleam in her eyes, however, told Cam the only thing she was sorry about was that sharing this news with her society friends would have to wait until she could get to a telephone.

Chapter Ten

They didn't stay for dinner. Cam canceled their meal orders and hustled a pale Maddie out the same door that Melinda had sashayed through just minutes earlier.

"Are you okay?" he asked once they were seated in his truck in the restaurant's brightly lit parking lot.

"How could he name his second child Michael?"

At an absolute loss for how to comfort her, Cam merely held her hand. "I don't know, sweetheart."

"Maybe it's his way of coping," she said, half to herself.

Cam found he couldn't hold his tongue, not when she was making excuses for something that, in his book, could not be excused. "Or maybe he's just a coldhearted jerk."

"No, Ted's not a bad person. The situation just makes him seem that way. He's still grieving a much-wanted child."

"Grieving? You're grieving, Maddie. But I don't think he is, at least not to the same extent, or he wouldn't have named this baby Michael, too."

"He wanted a son." In fact, Maddie recalled now how excited he'd been when an ultrasound had revealed the sex. He'd given her a sapphire bracelet and matching pendant. Blue, for a boy, he'd said. And then he'd told her that their boy would be named Michael. Michael Theodore Stewart IV.

"Michael is Ted's legal name. He uses the shortened version of his middle name to distinguish himself from his father and grandfather."

When Cam just stared at her, she murmured, "It's a family name."

"Yes, and it was already given to a family member. Children are precious gifts. They're individuals. They can't be replaced even if others come along for us to love after them."

She wiped away a tear. "Ted loved our son. I know he did. Afterward, after what I had done, he…he couldn't stand the sight of me. It was just too painful a reminder of what he had lost."

An heir, Cam thought uncharitably, recalling Melinda's words. "Yes. But he had no right to blame you."

"He did. It was my fault," she replied resolutely.

Cam decided to take another tack. "Were you drinking the night of your accident?"

Maddie's chin shot up and she felt her mouth fall open for a moment before she responded, "Of course not. I wouldn't drink and drive. My God, Cameron, I was six months pregnant."

He ignored her umbrage. "Were you speeding?"

"No. The roads were bad, so I was going well below the posted limit."

"You must not have been wearing a seat belt then."

"I always wear my seat belt," she replied indignantly.

"Ah," he nodded, stretching one arm out over the back of the seat. "You must have fallen asleep at the wheel."

She turned toward him, outrage and hurt warring for dominance. "How can you say that? You know I didn't. I told you, I saw those headlights coming at me. I still see them in my nightmares. It's not something I will ever forget."

Even as she waited for an apology, he glanced away. When he finally spoke again, the change in topic and the change in the tone of his voice confused Maddie.

"When Angie died, I felt it was my fault."

The quiet statement vanquished Maddie's irritation. "Why would you think such a thing? She had cancer."

"Yes, she did. But that didn't stop me from blaming myself for her death. I kept thinking, maybe if we'd tried one more experimental treatment or traveled to a clinic in Mexico that we'd heard about…" He waved his hand.

"If there were a bona fide cure for cancer, believe me, people wouldn't have to travel outside the United States to get it. There are a lot of quacks out there eager to prey on desperate people, Cameron."

"Today's quack might turn out to be tomorrow's Jonas Salk," he debated.

"Yes, or tomorrow's quack," she replied pointedly. Her tone was more gentle when she asked, "Were you loving and supportive when Angela needed you to be?"

"I never left her side."

She smiled. "Of course you didn't. You wouldn't. That's the kind of person you are." And one of the many reasons, she admitted to herself, that she'd fallen so hopelessly in love with him.

"So, you're saying I shouldn't blame myself for something I couldn't prevent?"

"Yes…" The light clicked on then. "It's not the same, Cameron."

"It's exactly the same. I couldn't prevent Angie's death, and the only way you could have prevented the accident that took your unborn son's life was if you hadn't been on the road at that very moment."

"I shouldn't have been. Ted told me not to go."

"It was an accident, Maddie. Who's to say something like it wouldn't have happened with Ted behind the wheel and you riding in the passenger seat? We don't get a heads-up before bad things happen. Don't you think you should cut yourself some slack?"

"My son is dead," she whispered.

"So is my wife. And there's nothing either of us can do to change that. We have to deal with it. We have to move forward." He glanced down at his hand, which gripped the steering wheel. "I took off my wedding band for good that night we were together, Maddie. I put it away with Angie's in a lockbox for Caroline to have someday. Do you want to know why?"

She couldn't speak. She couldn't seem to breathe. He took her silence for consent.

"I took it off because you were right. I'm alive, and I don't want to live the rest of my life alone. I want to share it with someone who will love and need Caroline and me as much as we love and need her. I think, Maddie, that I want to share it with—"

She stopped his words with one of her hands, desperate to cut him off. "I'm glad you're ready to move on, but it will have to be with someone else. I'm not right for you, Cameron."

He shook his head, slumped back in his seat. She thought she heard him mutter a mild oath before he turned to her and said, "That ex of yours certainly did a number on you. And you've certainly done a number on me."

"On you?"

"Yeah. You pushed me to feel again. And I feel plenty right now. I feel betrayed."

"Betrayed? How have I betrayed you?"

"You told me there could be someone special out there for me if I had the will and the courage to look. Well, I'm looking, Maddie. I'm looking right at you. And do you know what I see?"

She barely had time to shake her head before he barreled ahead. "I see a woman who despite all her fine speeches is nothing but a hypocrite."

That stung, but then Ted had once called her worse. She took the insult on the chin, and even reminded

Cameron, "Don't forget fraud. I believe you've called me that, too."

He sent her a scathing look, clearly not at all pleased with her help. "The least you could do is have the decency to practice what you preach."

"Oh, Cameron. You deserve so much more than I can give you." She sucked in a deep breath, released it before revealing the one thing that had made it so much easier for Ted to walk out on her. "I...I can't have children. Ever."

She expected that announcement to get a reaction from him and it certainly did—just not the one she'd anticipated.

"Oh, well, then, I guess I can't possibly love you." He reached out, grabbed her by the shoulders and gave her a little shake. "Is that all you think I'm looking for, some kind of brood mare? Do I look like Ted, like a man who sees you only as a means for producing an heir? I'm the last male in the Foley line. Sure, I would love more kids—girls, boys, whatever. But kids grow up, and if you've done your job right, they move out to live their own lives. I want someone who is going to grow old with me."

"I thought that you wouldn't...that you couldn't..." Her thoughts were too jumbled and erratic to allow her to finish.

"What does love mean to you, Maddie?"

She looked at him through the haze of her tears, and felt exactly like the hypocrite he'd accused her of being. The woman who owned a business named True Love, Incorporated was utterly at a loss. All of her old notions about men and women, commitment and intimacy had been torn asunder, shattered by Cameron's simple words and quiet conviction. "I...I don't know what it means."

She felt his hands slip from her shoulders to grasp her numb fingers. His voice was barely above a whisper, but no less forceful when he said, "Of course you don't, because when you needed someone to stand by you, he walked away. When you needed someone to accept you as you are, he couldn't or wouldn't. And when you needed someone to forgive you—even for something that wasn't your fault—he assigned you the blame instead. That's not love, Maddie."

"But Ted..."

Cam silenced her with a shake of his head. "Love means taking the bad with the good. It means working through the hard times together, as a team. The vows say it all, Maddie. For better or worse, in sickness and in health, for richer or poorer."

"I couldn't make them stick," she cried softly. Why wouldn't he understand?

"Maybe you could the second time around. With me."

She felt the air back up in her lungs. Any moment, she just knew he would be proposing. It thrilled her, even as it left her shaken. She had to think, and she couldn't do that sitting across from him in the intimate confines of the truck cab.

"My...my pager just went off," she blurted out. "I felt it vibrate against my hip."

Cameron expelled a sigh of frustration and rubbed his eyes with the thumb and index finger of his left hand. "Maddie, we're having an important conversation here. I think business can wait, especially since your office hours are long over for the day."

"Yes, but I'm expecting an important call from my parents," she fibbed as she riffled through her purse, pretending to hunt for her cellular. "Oh, no, my phone's not here." Another lie, she thought as her fingers brushed over its sleek surface.

"Perhaps it's in your briefcase," he said, his tone thick with impatience.

"No, I always keep it in my purse. What if it fell out when I put my purse under my chair in the restaurant?" She crossed her fingers that he wouldn't remember she'd hung her purse by its strap from the back of her chair.

"I'll go check," he grumbled. "But don't think this little reprieve gets you off the hook. This conversation isn't over. We've got things to settle."

Maddie waited until he disappeared inside the restaurant before she got out of the truck and hurried as best she could across the icy parking lot. Before her accident, she would have braved the bone-chilling cold and walked the three-quarters of a mile to her apartment. But she did the sensible thing and ducked inside a nearby pub to use the pay phone and call a cab. And all the while she berated herself as a coward. The man she had just run away from said he loved her. And it was clear that he wanted to marry her. It wasn't a question of loving him back. She did. Deeply, desperately. She loved him so much that she wanted what was best for him. Now she just had to decide exactly what—or who—that was.

* * *

Early the next morning, Maddie did something she hadn't done even after losing the baby or the finalization of her divorce. She called for a plane reservation, packed her bags and went home to Georgia. She needed the physical distance from Cameron to gain some perspective. But, that night, as she sat in the tastefully decorated front parlor of her parents' house working a crossword puzzle, Cameron Foley was very much on her mind.

"I swear, Madison, you're a million miles away. Why, I've been talking to you for more than five minutes, and I know you haven't heard a word I'm saying," Eliza chided. She was seated across the room from Maddie on the camelback sofa, sipping a cup of tea.

"Sorry, Mother. I have a lot on my mind."

"So I see." Eliza returned the cup to its saucer, stroked the delicately curved handle for a moment. "Do you want to talk about it?"

If Maddie hadn't been seated, her mother's unprecedented suggestion probably would have caused her to collapse on the floor in shock. As it was, she scratched the felt pen across the newspaper page, obliterating the boxes for seventeen across.

What had gotten into her mother? Eliza wasn't one to invite confidences. She preferred a relationship that was all smooth surface, rather than delving into the murky depths where life's problems could ruin a perfectly good mood.

Still, she appeared to be trying. Maddie decided to

grasp the extended olive branch. "I've met some-one."

"Oh? Another Northerner, I suppose."

Maddie couldn't suppress the chuckle. "Yes, Mother, Cameron Foley is a Yankee."

"Well, let's hope he's not another Ted."

Maddie felt her mouth drop open. This was the first even remotely disparaging comment Eliza had made about her daughter's ex-husband. Indeed, Maddie had taken her mother's abiding silence on the subject to mean she, too, felt Maddie deserved to be punished.

"I thought you liked Ted."

"I liked him fine, dear, until he left you lying in a hospital room, all broken like Humpty-Dumpty. Your father and I were sure if we just stayed away, gave you both time, he would come to his senses."

"But you never said anything. I thought…I thought you blamed me, too."

"Blamed you? For what, Madison?"

"For Michael's death."

"Why ever would you think such a thing? That was a tragedy, but hardly your fault."

"But you won't talk about it. Every time I've tried to bring up the subject, you've changed it. I just as-sumed…" She let the newspaper and pen fall to the floor. "I assumed you felt as Ted did. As I did. That I was to blame for my baby's death."

Her mother set the cup and saucer on the coffee table, and then crossed the room until she stood next to Maddie's chair. The hand she laid on Maddie's shoulder was hesitant, the slight pats awkward. And yet it was the sweetest moment Maddie could recall spending with her mother.

"Ted may have blamed you, but I certainly never did. Nor did your father. And neither should you blame yourself. It was an accident, Madison. A horrible, horrible accident. If I didn't talk about it, well, it was because I didn't know what to say." She sighed. "I'm not good with words. But I do love you and I do want you to be happy."

Maddie's breath hitched, but she willed back the tears, worried that a little saltwater might frighten her mother away. And she needed her now. She very much needed her. She squeezed her mother's hand. "I love you, too."

Eliza took the chair next to Maddie's. After crossing her ankles demurely and making a show of smoothing the material of her skirt over her knees, she said, "Now, why don't you tell me about your young man? What does he do?"

"Cameron is a cherry farmer."

"Ah, a cherry farmer." Eliza's lips pursed a moment and she sighed dramatically. "Well, I suppose if a peanut farmer is good enough to be president of the United States of America, a cherry farmer might be good enough for my daughter."

"He is, Mother. He loves me. Knowing everything, he loves me. And he wants to marry me." She whispered the words as though they were a secret.

Her mother smiled broadly. Not the plastic smile she usually offered, either. "Do you love him back?"

"More than I thought it was possible to love a man."

"Then why do you look so sad?"

"I want what's best for Cameron, Mother. His first wife, whom he loved deeply, died three years ago, and he has the most wonderful little girl. I promised to find him a match through my dating service. And I think I have. Her name is Peggy Modean, but I've been putting off introducing the two of them."

"It doesn't seem to me that he's interested in this Peggy Modean."

"That's only because he hasn't met her."

"No, dear, I'd say it's because *he* has met *you*."

Maddie mulled over her mother's words for the next few days, reevaluating everything, from her relationship with Ted to her son's death to her feelings for Cameron. Had she been wrong all these months? Had it been easier, she wondered, to wallow in guilt than to work through her grief? Did she deserve a second chance? With Cameron and Caroline? Or would they be better off with someone as seemingly perfect as Peggy Modean?

When she finally had her answers, Maddie boarded an airplane and headed back to Michigan.

"Hello, Cameron," she said when he answered the telephone early Friday morning.

"Maddie." The relief she heard turned to irritation when he added, "That was quite a disappearing act you pulled the other night."

"I apologize for that." She coiled the telephone cord around her index finger, glad he couldn't witness her show of nerves. "I needed time to think."

"Yeah, and what have you come up with?"

"We'll save that for another conversation, if you don't mind. This is really a business call. I have a date for you. Tonight. The notice is short, but that couldn't be helped."

"Maddie, I do mind. I don't want to go out on any more dates." Frustration and more than a little disappointment colored his tone.

Talking over the mild oath that followed, she reminded him, "We had a deal."

"Why are you doing this? What are you hoping to prove?"

She ignored the questions. "It's against our policy really, but you'll have to pick up your date at her home."

"I'm not picking anyone up anywhere," he said stubbornly.

But Maddie rattled off an address, anyway.

"I think she's perfect for you," she said, and then to Cam's angry astonishment, she hung up.

Still fuming, Cam strode through the door of True Love, Incorporated late that afternoon. He'd done this before, he realized. Twice. Gone in to confront Maddie Daniels with temper raised and guns blazing. And look where it had gotten him—in love and out of patience. Well, this time there would be no cute bargains struck. He was getting what he wanted or he was walking out heavyhearted. But at least the matter would be settled.

Lisa sat at the reception desk, filing a blue-painted fingernail. She offered a saccharine smile as he started past her desk. "Don't bother. Miss Daniels isn't here. She won't be back today. Oh, and if you, like, plan to spend half the night in the waiting room again, I'll warn you that the bathroom sink is only giving out cold water." She smirked. "But then maybe that's what you need."

He ignored the jibe, which was too accurate for his comfort. As irritating as it was to find Maddie gone, he did have another matter to take care of.

"I'm supposed to go on a date tonight. Maddie just gave me an address, no phone number and no name. I'm not going on that date."

Lisa stopped filing and inclined her head. "Really, that's too bad. You should. The woman Miss Daniels picked out is, like, perfect for you. You know, stubborn and thickheaded. Has to do things her own way."

Cam leaned forward over the desk, adding a little menace to his tone. "Look, I need to cancel."

Surly seemed to work. Lisa's eyes went wide and she nodded in agreement. "Sure, Mr. Foley, I'll get right on that."

His smug attitude lasted all of five seconds. She glanced at the clock and rose with a shrug. "Sorry. It's five o'clock. My workday is done. You'll have to come back on Monday morning if you want that information."

"The date is tonight," he replied between gritted teeth.

She dumped the emery board into her small backpack of a purse. "Bummer."

Muttering curses, Cam stalked to his truck. He had
no intention of going on this blind date, but he
couldn't very well leave the woman hanging. After
all, it wasn't her fault that she'd found herself in the
middle of this mess. She was an innocent third party.
He pulled the crumpled paper from the pocket of his
jeans and noted the address. It wasn't far. He could
stop by and explain the situation, offer an apology,
and be home in time to order a pepperoni pizza with
Caroline.

Five minutes later, he stood outside an apartment
door, hoping his mystery date would be the understanding sort. He knocked soundly, shifted from foot
to foot, rehearsing in his head what he would say.
When he heard the dead bolt slide free, he cleared his
throat. Then the door swung open and he simply forgot how to breathe.

Maddie stood on the other side of the threshold,
her mass of dark hair waving around her face like a
flag of surrender. That quirky mole was raised along
with one speculative eyebrow. For the first time since
he'd met her, she wore a dress. Not just any dress,
but a short, black, curve-hugging sheath with thin
straps at the shoulders. The scars were visible if one
chose to look. Cam didn't see them. He saw only
Maddie Daniels, the woman he loved, glowing with
health, smiling with promise.

"It's you," he whispered in disbelief.

"It's me."

"I thought…I came here to break the date. I figured this was just another setup."

"It almost was," she admitted. "I had a woman

picked out for you. Peggy Modean. I've had her picked out for quite some time, but I kept putting off introducing the two of you, because I thought she would be your perfect match."

"You're my perfect match. I don't want Peggy Modean."

She closed her eyes briefly, opened them on a smile. "I was hoping you'd say that. I was *really* hoping you'd say that." There was a hint of vulnerability beneath her words when she added, "I was worried you might have changed your mind about me. I've given you plenty of reasons to."

"I haven't changed my mind. You might not have realized it, but you've also given me plenty of reasons *not* to." He stepped across the threshold and pulled her into his arms. Home, he thought, I've just come home.

Maddie melted against him with a soft sigh, and just before his mouth closed over hers, she whispered the three little words that made his heart sing and his spirits soar.

"I love you, too," he told her when the kiss ended. "All of you. You're beautiful, Maddie. Inside and out."

She seemed ready to protest, but then she smiled instead. "You make me feel beautiful."

"And you make me feel alive. For the first time in years, I'm excited about the future."

Maddie didn't think anyone had ever paid her a higher compliment. She took Cam's beloved face between her hands and kissed him again until they were both a little breathless. Afterward, as she waited for her blood to cool, she fiddled with the zipper on his leather jacket and reminded him, "You know, according to our deal, on the second date you have to wear a tie and bring me roses. A dozen, I believe. Long-stemmed and red."

"I'm afraid I can't do that."

"You can't?"

"Nope." Cam pulled back so he could look her square in the eye. "On the second date, Madison Daniels, I'm going to wear a tuxedo. And forget about roses, I'll bring you orange blossoms instead."

"Cameron," she sighed, smiling around her tears. They were the happiest she could remember shedding.

"You know, I don't think I can wait very long to make you mine for keeps." His hands skimmed up her arms to finger the thin straps of her dress. He tugged one aside, letting it fall off her shoulder. Then he dropped a kiss where it had been and began working his way up her neck. Between nibbles, he said, "So, what are you doing next Saturday?"

Maddie knew what he was asking, and she didn't need to think about it this time. She pulled him farther inside the apartment, nearer to her heart. The door she closed behind him also sealed shut the past.

"I'm starting over," she said simply. "I'm starting over with you and Caroline."

* * * * *

SILHOUETTE *Romance*™

**Lost siblings, secret worlds,
tender seduction—live the fantasy in...**

A
TALE
OF THE
SEA

**Separated and hidden since childhood,
Phoebe, Kai, Saegar and Thalassa
must reunite in order to safeguard
their underwater kingdom.
But who will protect *them*...?**

July 2002
MORE THAN MEETS THE EYE
by Carla Cassidy (SR #1602)

August 2002
IN DEEP WATERS
by Melissa McClone (SR #1608)

September 2002
CAUGHT BY SURPRISE
by Sandra Paul (SR #1614)

October 2002
FOR THE TAKING
by Lilian Darcy (SR #1620)

*Look for these titles wherever
Silhouette books are sold!*

Silhouette®

™ *Where love comes alive*™

SRTOS

**Where royalty and romance
go hand in hand...**

The series continues in Silhouette Romance
with these unforgettable novels:

HER ROYAL HUSBAND
by Cara Colter
on sale July 2002 (SR #1600)

THE PRINCESS HAS AMNESIA!
by Patricia Thayer
on sale August 2002 (SR #1606)

SEARCHING FOR HER PRINCE
by Karen Rose Smith
on sale September 2002 (SR #1612)

And look for more Crown and Glory stories in
SILHOUETTE DESIRE starting in October 2002!

Available at your favorite retail outlet.

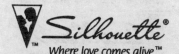

eHARLEQUIN.com

community | membership

buy books | authors | online reads | magazine | learn to write

buy books

Your one-stop shop for great reads at great prices. We have all your favorite Harlequin, Silhouette, MIRA and Steeple Hill books, as well as a host of other bestsellers in Other Romances. Discover a wide array of new releases, bargains and hard-to-find books today!

learn to write

Become the writer you always knew you could be: get tips and tools on how to craft the perfect romance novel and have your work critiqued by professional experts in romance fiction. Follow your dream now!

Silhouette®

Where love comes alive™—online...

Visit us at
www.eHarlequin.com

SILHOUETTE *Romance*

COMING NEXT MONTH